CW00421981

Kath Middleton began her word stories) and contribu Hill's second drabble collec she moved up a size to contribute short stories to anthologies. Shortly afterwards, she progressed to writing longer pieces and already she has a considerable back catalogue of acclaimed work. Kath likes to put her characters in difficult situations and watch them work their way out. She believes in the indomitable nature of the human spirit (and chickens). Kath is retired. She graduated in geology and has a certificate in archaeology. When she's in a hole, she doesn't stop digging.

A Note from the Author

Major to Minor is a collection of some of my short stories. They vary in length and in genre. One or two have been published before, and in those cases I credit the original publications at the end of the book. Some were written especially for the UK Crime Book Club, a Facebook group of over 26,000 members, mainly readers (although writers are readers too). The group has four events per year in which people, whether published authors or not, are offered the chance to write a story to be published in the group. It's always great fun and I'm addicted to writing these UKCBC SHORTS.

Published by Hilltop Press
Cover image painted by Aly Shaw
Cover design by Jonathan Hill

ISBN: 9798864835357

MAJOR TO MINOR

Kath Middleton

HAVE A WONDERFUL
CHRISTMAS 2023

love from Kath
x

Summertime

And the living is easy, or so they say. Me and Jack were teaming up and things were looking rosy. He was fresh out after his last stretch of pleasuring Her Majesty. Trouble with Jack is, he's never heard the phrase 'be prepared'. He's always the one who does something stupid and gets caught. Me, I'm the opposite. I like to run even the simplest burglary like a military operation. Planning, that's the name of the game. I see myself as a career criminal. Jack's just a career wally but he's light and nippy and has his uses.

"It's gonna be a doddle," I say to him. "Summer time, hot spell of weather, what do they all do?"

"Erm… oh, go on their holidays?"

"Well yeah, obviously. But their gaffs are all locked up tighter than a nun's, erm, tighter than anything. Alarms, big gates, them WiFi things that watch your house for you."

"So why are we…"

I honestly couldn't bear to listen to the rusty clanking of the two little brain cells knocking together in that noggin of his. "Jack, my laddo, what they does is, they goes to bed all hot and sweaty and they leaves the windows open! They might have swanky window locks but it's the hot weather that defeats them."

Honest, it was like watching a slow sunrise to see it dawn

on him, soft lad that he is.

"So then we sneak in and relieve them of their expensive possessions," I continued. "Not many people have cash around these days, but their houses are dripping with all that electronic stuff. Laptops, tablets, mobile phones, no end of good swag."

"Jewellery and that?" he asked.

"See, that'll be upstairs – bedroom, office – in a safe. We want what we can grab from downstairs and leg it."

Jack was all for going at it like a bull at a gate. We'd chosen a posh estate, but I wanted to have an evening recce. The hot weather was forecast to continue for another day or two so I wanted to see which houses had the windows open at night.

We'd do the actual job at two in the morning. I always thought that was the sweet spot 'cos that's when they move the clocks back or forward an hour. Stands to reason they wouldn't do it when people was out and about. See, Jack would never even give that a thought. But just to suss out the place, we needed to be around when they were going to bed. See who left what windows open where, kinda thing.

At 9.30 that night, we drove to the gates – it was one of them gated developments. A little stream ran close by so we followed that and in a few hundred yards the path ran behind the gardens. I knew that from Google Earth. I've got it up here, me.

I'd finally convinced Jack we weren't going in tonight. Just a recce. He was dead fidgety though. We chose a property at the end of a cul-de-sac to keep an eye on. Mainly 'cos it had a slightly lower fence. Well, a trellis really. Lucky for us it had all sweet peas and stuff climbing up it instead of thorny roses. We climbed over it, no bother, and sussed out the house. Right swanky, it was.

I'm not an idiot, though. I knew they'd have burglar alarms, but people often get complacent. They don't bother setting them when they're in the house. The key pads are usually in the hallway so we crept up and I watched through me binoculars. No curtains drawn 'cos it was still barely dark, especially if you'd got your night vision, like we had. It was our first house, and my luck was in. The lights were on in the downstairs rooms, and over the next hour or two, first teenaged kids, then adults, trooped up the stairs, passing the key pad on the hall wall. I could see it clearly. Nobody touched it. Money for old rope tomorrow night. And teenagers have loads of electronics. We'd be quids in.

They had security lights, of course, but I could see the ones round the back here were over the patio doors. No worries. We'd got our eyes on the window of a utility room round the side. Doddle.

The next night was even hotter. Dead close and sweaty, sultry even. See, Jack wouldn't even know that word. Still, he had his uses. At around quarter to two, we scaled the sweet pea trellis, "Don't go near that security light," I said to Jack, "and we'll be okay."

We snuck around the little side path to the utility room door. There was a window next to it and yes, the top part was open. Jack's a skinny lad so I gave him a leg up to climb through it.

Suddenly there was a flash of lightning that showed Jack stuck half way through the window, and the householder standing facing us in the utility room. He was wearing some silky bathrobe effort and he had a glass of milk in his hand. He dropped the glass, made a grab for Jack, and at that moment there was a deep crash of thunder and the heavens opened. It was coming down like a waterfall. I was drenched in seconds. I mean, what else could I do? He'd got Jack bang to rights, but no reason he should get us both. Just our damned bad luck that the bloke should fancy a glass of milk at two in the morning! I did a runner before the police arrived.

So much for my summer nights theory. They say the British summer is two fine days and a thunderstorm. They got that right. I might have to take an unexpected holiday myself. I wouldn't put it past that daft eejit Jack to dob me in it. Ho hum. The best laid plans and all that.

The Dark Lady

Liz Halstead was bursting with excitement as she collected the keys to her new flat. New wasn't really the word as it was the ground floor of a Victorian town house split into three. It was new to her, and it was the first flat she didn't have to share with others.

She pushed the key into the lock and twisted it. There was a small lobby which gave onto her own front door, and a staircase up to the other flats. Second key in hand, she unlocked the door to her own realm. Her space. She was pleased that the landlord had kept the tiling of the hallway floor, which screamed old-world elegance. To the left was the door to her living room. She pushed it open and went in. She'd been in before, of course, to look around, but not to be able to twirl in the centre of the empty room and think, 'All mine,' as she did now.

The room behind, probably called a parlour in its day, was her bedroom. It was slightly odd in shape as a corner had been made into a small en-suite bathroom. The rooms were large enough to do this without making her bedroom poky. Beyond, at the end of the hall, was a long, narrow kitchen. Although the flat was bare of furniture, the kitchen had come fully equipped. All Liz needed to do was get her possessions delivered from her old, shared flat, and buy a few new pieces.

Then it would be home.

Over the next weeks Liz fitted out the flat, with a few big, bright posters to make shining oases in the desert of magnolia walls. In her living room, however, she was unable to remove the massive, full-length oval mirror. It seemed to have been built into the room and was tightly cemented to the wall. Its ornate frame, a dark and looming mahogany presence, dominated that wall and no amount of surrounding it with bright prints could draw the eye away from it.

Whenever Liz moved around in the front room, she seemed to catch a quick movement in the mirror, even though she was not standing close enough to see her own reflection. She tried to concentrate on the dark shape flitting through her field of vision. It looked like a woman in a long, black dress. As soon as she approached to look into it deeply, she could only see her own reflection. It was a bit unnerving.

She tapped the mirror but it was solidly fixed in place. The glass was good quality. It didn't distort as you moved closer or farther away. There was no accounting for the flitting figure she was certain she could see. Those glimpses indicated a tall, slender young woman with long, dark hair, not unlike hers. As soon as Liz tried for a closer look, the image was replaced by her own. It worked just like a mirror should, and showed behind her the bright, stylish room she'd created from a bare, chilly space.

Right at the end of October, with the rain blasting at her as soon as she leapt from her car, Liz hurriedly pushed the keys into their locks, turned on the lights and raised the heating. She'd never been so glad to get in from work. The weather was vile and the journey home had been a nightmare. It was dark early in the afternoon at this time of year but today it had never seemed to get light.

She hung up her coat, dripping after the short sprint from the parking area behind the flats, and turned up the gas fire in the living room, trying to stop her teeth from chattering. She was frozen, and could see her breath like a misty curtain before her eyes.

After a quick detour to the kitchen to make a hot drink, Liz dropped onto her sofa and kicked off her shoes. The gas fire was starting to take the chill off the air but she still huddled over her drink, sipping it slowly. The evening meal could wait. She felt her shoulders, tense until now, begin to fall and relax. Home. You couldn't beat it on a night like this.

Eventually she rose to draw the heavy curtains and shut out the night and the rain, battering like pebbles on the windows. As she turned, she caught the usual black shape shifting in the mirror. "Come on, whoever you are," she challenged. "Let's see you." She walked over to stand right in front of the polished glass. There. Only her own reflection looking back at her.

Slowly, so gradually she wasn't aware of what was happening, the image in the mirror resolved into the dark lady, of whom she had only caught glimpses until now. The woman bore a startling resemblance to her own reflection in the mirror. It was like looking at herself in period costume. The woman's eyes challenged hers, seemingly from a mere few feet away. Liz could observe the strangely stiff black dress, the long skirt sweeping the floor. They shifted about, one then the other image dominant. The woman's hair was long, dark and loose, like hers, but a veil or shawl covered the top. She looked like a woman in mourning, sad, red eyes and glistening cheeks.

The images stopped shifting about, eventually, and Liz could see nothing of herself or her own living room in the dark reflection. The woman, so like her, moved closer to the mirror, as if straining to see an image in there. As she did so, Liz felt herself impelled to move in closer too. A flash – of what? Pleasure, desire, greed? The eyes of the woman in the mirror lit from within. Liz was drawn closer. She was afraid now, and tried to pull away. She couldn't. Her nose was now inches from that of the woman she stared at. She closed her eyes but the image remained, seemingly burnt into her retinas. Liz knew she was still being drawn forward and opened her eyes again. The woman, her twin in looks, was so close now, nose to nose, it was a wonder she couldn't hear her breathing.

And then she could. Breathing and whispering – "Come to me. Come closer."

Another voice, that of a man, said, "Mary, for goodness' sake come away from that mirror."

Liz felt the scream bubble up in her throat as she and the woman swept forward till they seemed to occupy the same space, the same body – and it was really cold. Icy cold. They each moved forward again, and with what felt like a sharp tug, they seemed to pass through each other. She had gone through the mirror, and so had the woman. Behind her she heard a tinkle of laughter, like glass shattering into tiny shards, but when she turned, the mirror was intact, though it still showed the other woman whose eyes were now shining in pleasure and triumph.

Liz took another step forward into a room just like the one she had left. Long, stiff skirts moved around her ankles. The room looked like her own, safe living room, but differently furnished. Those in there with her wore old-fashioned clothing. It was like a tableau in a museum. There was an old woman in a chair by the fire. She rocked and keened and dabbed her eyes with a lacy handkerchief. An elderly man in a frock coat leant on the mantelpiece, head in hands. On a central table, resting on a deep red velvet cloth, was an open coffin containing a younger man, hands folded over his chest, and waxen in death.

A knock at the front door startled them. The old man

roused himself as a figure in a dark blue uniform stalked into the room with an air of authority. He looked around him, taking in the scene. Then he marched straight up to Liz and said, "Mary Taylor?" Liz shook her head in denial, unable to believe what was happening to her. "I am arresting you for the murder of your husband, George Taylor, evilly done away with by means of poison." He rested his hand upon the coffin, glancing briefly at the pale young man within. "You will come with me to be incarcerated until your trial."

She had changed places, changed lives with a woman who resembled her in every detail, and walked into the responsibility for that other woman's actions. They were the image of one another. Who would believe her story? She turned to the mirror behind her, showing her in dark formal clothing in this Victorian room. She placed her hands flat on the cold glass, banging on it. "Come back!" she cried. "Come back!"

"Mary," said the older man. "I've told you to leave that mirror alone. Haven't you done enough damage… to our son? To our lives?"

As the police officer grasped her by the arm and she was led away, Liz appeared to be the only one who could hear, over the impossible distance of years, that tinkling laugh.

The Moths

Uncle John was a keen moth-trapper. He'd taken it up when he took early retirement through ill-health. Superficially he looked very well, but he'd had a heart attack and was on a lot of medication. Still, they'd told him at the hospital that he had to take exercise, so he managed to rent an allotment nearby and kept most of the family in fresh vegetables.

He had a set-up for the moths that shone a light at night, and they came to it, as is their nature. They would go inside the trap, then settle down on the egg-boxes he put in there, to give them cover and shelter. Next day, he'd open the trap, count the numbers and species, take their photographs and note it all down in his Moth Book. He'd cover the trap with an old teatowel, put it in a cool, shady spot, then the following night, he'd let them go. I once asked him why he never trapped on consecutive nights. "Because I might trap the same ones again and they'd not get chance to feed," he said.

One Saturday towards the end of the school summer holidays, he and I were out on his allotment, lifting his potatoes, when he made an odd noise. I looked up and saw he'd gone a strange, grey colour. "What is it, Uncle John? Is it your heart again?"

He struggled to nod his head and I didn't know what to

do. I was just a schoolboy and, although I'd done a first aid course, this was beyond my skill set. At that point he fell to the ground and, checking his pulse, I found none. I pulled out my phone and rang 999. The responder said an ambulance was on its way and reminded me how to do chest compressions with occasional breaths. It would feel seriously weird breathing into my uncle's mouth.

I rolled Uncle John on his back, and began fiercely pumping at his chest, over the heart. His eyes were closed, his lips turning blue and he wasn't breathing. I was scared to death.

Suddenly my vision shuddered as a cloud of moths flew in front of my face. They landed on Uncle John, on his face, in his hair, on his old gardening jacket. They were large, hairy and made me shudder. Although I knew he loved them, moths gave me the creeps, especially close up like this. I didn't dare touch them. They had hairy bodies and their wings occasionally shivered in a disconcerting way. I'd never been so close to them before, and certainly not so many of them. I jumped back for a moment, but knew I had to steel myself to go back to the compressions. As I pushed on his chest, the little furry bodies rose and fell too. I was seriously creeped out, but my uncle's life could depend on me not being a wuss and daring to put my hands close to those moths.

Then, after the count, I had to breathe into his mouth till his chest inflated. Could I do it? The moths on his face were the biggest, and there were loads of them. As I tentatively approached his mouth with mine, the moths seemed to shuffle back a bit, as though to give me room. I felt the slight tickle from a wing or two, but I managed to do it.

Then I heard John speak to me. His voice wasn't coming from his lips, but dropped, like a falling leaf into a still pond, straight into my mind, setting up similar ripples. "Press harder," he said. "Harder! And breathe harder."

I wanted to scream, but I had to remind myself that my uncle's death was more of a screaming matter than touching a moth. And where had they all come from in the middle of the morning like this? With hands filthy from lifting potatoes, I shoved on his chest with my whole weight, and on the count of thirty I put my mouth over his again, and huffed as hard as I could.

Eventually, and it felt like years but it could have been ten or fifteen minutes, two paramedics rushed across the allotment site. One took over from me and the other asked me questions. Some of them were about the moths, though one by one they'd begun flittering off, and some were about how long I'd been doing the compressions. Too long, I thought to myself. I was knackered. And how long could he go on without breathing by himself?

Gradually the moths dispersed, leaving Uncle John's face dirty with my fingerprints, but clear of insects. One of the paramedics opened a box she'd been carrying. It turned out to be a portable defibrillator as I found out afterwards. They gave him several electric shocks then he seemed to spasm, arch his back and take in a deep breath of his own. The first for twenty minutes or so.

"Will he be okay?" I asked, while the paramedics continued to work, but I could see the colour coming back to my uncle's face as they did so.

"I think you've saved his life," said the one putting her defibrillator away. "Many people don't press hard enough. We always say it doesn't matter if you break a rib, so long as you get the heart functioning again. Well done."

They took John away in an ambulance and let me go with him, as the nearest available relative. I was dying to ask him about the moths but that had to wait. When he was about to be discharged with an additional lot of medication, he sat on the end of the hospital bed and I sat in the chair beside it. "Tell me about the moths, Uncle John," I said.

"You saw them?" he asked, looking a little puzzled.

"Of course," I said. "They were all over you, especially your face. I had to almost touch them to breathe for you. It was beyond creepy!"

"And did they let you hear me speak?" he asked.

That struck me as a very odd way of putting it. "Well, I heard you telling me to push harder, and to breathe harder. But your lips didn't move."

"They did that," he said. "The moths. They let me speak. I was on the brink. About to pass through the veil. But they can go in and out, you know. In many cultures there's a mythology about moths that involves the underworld, or the spirit world, as we might call it. It seems they were friendly towards me and allowed me to speak directly to you. They don't usually, but there are stories…"

"Well if anyone was a friend to moths, that would be you," I said.

Laughing, he reached out a hand for me to pull him up from the bed, and we walked out of the hospital. My mum was outside, waiting in the car, and the three of us went home together. He never spoke about the moths again, though he lived another fifteen years, and neither did I. But I've wondered. Oh yes, I've wondered…

Neighbours

Paul inserted the key in the door lock with a huge grin. Turning it, he pushed the door back and stepped into the small hall of his new apartment. It was only new to him, of course. The block had been here for years but this was his first own front door.

Living at home, his only private space had been his bedroom. As a child, that was as much as he wanted. Growing up, of course, he realised how little privacy his bedroom door gave him. His parents would knock before they came in, but his mother was in every day, tidying up, cleaning, changing linen. It was his space in name only.

Things looked up when he went to college. He had a room of his own with a lock. It wasn't that he was up to no good but everyone needs to feel they have somewhere on which they can put their own mark, and where they needn't wear their mask. Their outside face. *This place is mine. Come in only as an invited guest.*

Now, in a new town, ready to take up his first job, Paul had collected his keys with some excitement. He'd viewed the apartment, but only as an outsider. Now it would be home. He strode across the expanse of the wood floor, past the few bland furnishings that came with the place, and stood before the window. He was on the twelfth floor and had a view over to a similar block across the street.

The apartment had a good sized bedroom and a bathroom, though the kitchen and dining area were part of the living room. It was as large as he could afford and, for a single man, had more than enough space.

The window where he stood was above the kitchen sink and food preparation area. He leaned on the worktop and looked out. He could see, beyond the block in front of him, a small park. It was good to see trees in an area otherwise built up, and he told himself he'd go running there when he'd settled in and got into a work routine.

Once he got to know a few workmates, he hoped not to be spending too much time in this apartment. His image of big town life was of calling at a pub after work with his friends, maybe eating out with them, finally chilling in front of his television for an hour or so before bed. He wouldn't bother choosing artwork for the bland, mushroom-coloured walls, because he had no intention of spending any time looking at them.

The job was great. He enjoyed it, felt on top of the work and could hardly believe they were actually paying him for something he'd do free, if necessary. His other image of working life, though, fell a good deal short. Unlike entering college, where all the students were strangers to one another, and everyone eager to make friends, he felt he was intruding himself into established groups. They, while friendly, were wary, he could see. Softly, softly. Still, he often found himself in a pub alone, or giving in and coming home. This necessitated frozen or take-away food for dinner. He could almost hear his mum's voice in his head, asking him where the vegetables were, and was he going to have a piece of fruit after that.

The park running, early in the morning before work, was no doubt preventing him from piling on the weight, but he felt he was slipping into a bachelor life. And he was lonely.

His only contacts outside of work were a few of his neighbours with whom he would exchange a morning or evening greeting. Dorothy lived in one of the ground floor apartments and kept an eye out for everyone. An elderly lady, she didn't seem to have much else in her life, but she was friendly and it was great to have someone welcome him home at the end of the day. The man in the apartment directly below his was called Michael, he eventually discovered. 'Call me Mike,' he said, thrusting a hand out to shake Paul's. Mike didn't seem to be at home much and, from his clothing, was a fellow jogger, or perhaps a gym member.

As Paul stood at his kitchen worktop one afternoon, people-watching on the pavement below, he caught a flash of movement from the apartment directly opposite his. There were blinds up at the windows, but he and the person opposite had them raised to let in the evening light. He caught a bent head, blonde and curly, and a swift chopping movement from the blur of hands. A woman, preparing a meal, just as his mum used to, back home.

He felt a swift heart-punch of home-sickness, followed by the knowledge that he was easily capable of doing this for himself. He could prepare his own meals from fresh produce, just as his mum had done at home. Just as this young woman opposite was doing. After all, what else had he to spend his time on? He decided he'd buy the ingredients for a casserole the following day on his way back from work. There'd be plenty of time for it to cook while he caught up with a bit of television.

He came in with a bag of groceries that included a package of beef. Standing by the window, preparing them, slicing and chopping, he watched his neighbour opposite doing the self-same thing. Every so often she lifted her chopping board to slide the ingredients into some pot or pan just out of view. He found it hypnotic to watch her chop and slide, chop and slide, as she prepared the meal he couldn't see.

They worked in a harmony known only to him. He had some recollection of watching his mother, and began to fry the onions and stir in his beef strips before adding everything else, seasonings and stock. Banging the lid on tight, he transferred the cast iron pot to the oven and left it to cook. He couldn't help checking on the woman's progress, though. She was at the stage of attacking her meat with a cleaver. By golly, she meant business. She seemed dainty but strong, the muscles bunching in her slender arms as she hacked at it.

Paul got into the habit of making his own fresh meals, always in the unwitting company of the lady opposite. It made him feel a little uncomfortable, as though he were a stalker. He paid attention to what she chopped, though, and came to the conclusion that it wasn't always a one-pot dish, as he'd been making. Sometimes she chopped salads, sometimes vegetable accompaniments to a steak or a roast dinner. It made him determined to be more adventurous.

Shortly after he began on his culinary adventures, the local news channel reported the third in a series of murders in the area. He'd a vague recollection of hearing about an earlier one, but now there were three, all of the same kind, the police and the press were calling the perpetrator a serial killer. He sat on the couch, eating his latest home-cooked meal, when he lost his appetite.

"The killer appears to be targeting early morning or late evening joggers in local parks," said the newsreader. "The police are warning people to go in pairs or groups, for exercise. Rich Stuart, the reporter who broke the story, stated that the killer chooses strong, fit people and appears to hamstring them so they can't run away. They are then dragged into the bushes and killed with a swift blow to the throat, almost severing the neck. Then, and this is the unusual aspect of this case, he or she cuts off a leg and takes it away. The corpse is left with one leg and a slashed throat. Police are reluctant to speculate about this but Stuart vouches for its truth."

That could have been him, Paul realised. The newscaster went on to add, "There is no evidence to show where the missing limbs have been taken. Police are baffled." They'd like that, Paul thought. Making them sound incompetent.

He and his lady opposite continued their cooking activities. It always made him smile when he saw she was using similar ingredients to his. He must contrive to meet her some time. He knew which floor she lived on, but he rarely saw her leave or enter her building. Her work times and his evidently didn't coincide.

Then came the news that the caretaker in a neighbouring block had found part of a butchered human femur in the rubbish container outside. DNA had confirmed that it had belonged to one of the murdered men. Everyone in that block was subjected to a grilling from the police but nobody could be linked to the case. As some of them said, why would they dump the evidence by their own door? That would be stupid and someone who had got away with three of these killings was evidently not stupid.

The press went to town, calling the murders 'The Cannibal Killings'. The police were quoted as saying there was no evidence the flesh had been eaten, other than it had been cut from the bone. That didn't stop the local paper from producing a special edition with a red banner proclaiming the Cannibal Killer was at large in the area.

It made everyone edgy. Paul wanted to find someone to go out with in the mornings but didn't feel he knew Mike well enough to ask, though he occasionally saw him leaving or returning from a run. Joe, one of his workmates, lived nearby and they arranged to meet up and run together. It was a scary time, realizing that anyone you passed, or saw in the distance in the park, could be the killer. Many ran with backpacks, on their way to work, with a change of clothing and their lunchbox inside. Any one of those could contain a cleaver. It was horrible to find you suspected everyone.

Back home, Paul would settle to his soothing food preparation, once again fascinated by his neighbour opposite. The news, his work mate Joe, the water-cooler chat, all led him to be suspicious. He hated the way his mind worked but hadn't realized what an obsession this had become until the fears began to invade his dreams.

On two or three occasions he woke in the night in a tangle of sweaty sheets, his heart racing and the wisps of a fading dream telling him he'd been running from an attacker wielding a cleaver. He'd been the next victim of the Cannibal Killer. The first time it happened he was so terrified he found it impossible to sleep again. The adrenaline coursing through his system stoked him, brought him to instant wakefulness and sent his mind off in a flurry of anxious scenarios.

In this latest dream, he'd been running to escape, and had tripped. With a clutching feeling inside, he knew he was doomed. He felt the bite of the cleaver in his leg and screamed as he sat up in bed, grabbing his calf. It was cramp, but the dream had been so vivid. What had been worse, though, was that he'd caught a glimpse of his attacker as he tried to sprint to safety. Jumping at him from the shelter of a bush was the woman opposite. The cleaver she wielded was the small chopper he'd seen her use on meat and tough vegetables in the kitchen across the road. He had conflated two of his current obsessions, the murders, and the girl he watched each day, and the result was that he began to suspect even her.

He couldn't sleep more that night. He got up and showered, dressed for his usual run, but wondered if he should text Joe and cancel. If he did that, though, Joe would lose his run. People were scared now. Truly afraid for their lives. A fourth victim had been found and the news was that the murders were coming closer together. The killer was ramping it up. It was probably addictive, he thought. After the first death, the rest came easier. Surely he'd make a mistake soon and be caught.

He met with Joe at the park for their usual run, and told him he'd had a dream about the killer. "Me too," Joe admitted. "First time it was my boss at work! He's a killer for sure. Then it was someone in my block I've never got on with. I know it's playing on everyone's mind at the moment. My dreams seem to suggest I want it to be someone I already don't like."

"I get that, I suppose." Paul upped his pace to keep up with Joe, who was racing ahead now. "But in my dream it was someone I don't really know. I see her regularly but we've never actually met."

"What's this? You're a Peeping Tom now?" Joe slowed, panting as he started to laugh. "And how can it be a woman? Would they have the strength to butcher a corpse?"

Paul shivered at the thought, taking the opportunity to catch his own breath. "Perhaps, perhaps not. But you get women who work out and you get weedy men who are slobs. I don't think we can say for sure. It's made me feel horribly uncomfortable, though. I mean, I see her most days, from the other side of the street, and, if I'm honest, I'm rather attracted to her. But now – I just don't know. Let's be honest, it's only because we've been running together that I don't suspect you!"

For the rest of the week, Paul couldn't shake the fear that his neighbour opposite was cutting up human flesh. Sometimes he couldn't take his eyes from her window, but at others he was repulsed and couldn't bear to look. Why did she never look across to his window? He watched her but she seemed totally indifferent to him. Was it guilt? Did she refuse to acknowledge another's gaze because she knew what she was doing was wrong? Or was she just shy? His own mother would have said it was ill-mannered to stare at someone else as he did at her. She was probably simply better brought-up. And yet…

He found himself studying other joggers, particularly those with a back-pack. Could he see a knife-handle? Were there blood stains? It made him a tedious companion for Joe, lost as he was in his thoughts. Joe didn't seem inclined to be chatty either. On a couple of occasions he saw Mike, though he was usually returning home at that point. No machete handle or blood stains on his back pack. He thought the killer would be covered in blood. It couldn't be happening on a casual, early morning run, could it?

What was his girl opposite chopping up? He realised he didn't know what human meat looked like. He assumed, from the redness of the blood, that the leg meat would look like the beef he sometimes put in his casserole. Rich, dark and red, cooking to an unctuous brown, with lots of gravy. He was making himself feel sick with these thoughts. As a result, he'd taken to cooking chicken and fish more often.

The girl over the road was currently slicing pork. Preparing a stir-fry, from the look of things. He felt a lump forming in his throat, then dropping like lead to his stomach. Didn't they say human flesh tasted like pork? Long Pig, he'd heard it called. Oh, God! Was she slicing human flesh? Did it look as well as taste like pork? When was the last killing? Three days ago. And beef was often hung for weeks before it was ready to eat. Pork, or human leg, would last longer than three days. What did she have in her fridge? Could she freeze it? It would last weeks, months, if she did. But the Cannibal Killer was speeding up. Was she eating more meat? Fewer salads? He hadn't noticed. And perhaps the point of the killings was simply the power of life and death over another human being, not just the eating. The feasting on the meat was a by-product. Another benefit, if you looked at it like that. Waste not, want not.

After four months of living there, of watching the girl and lately wondering what she was chopping and fearing finding out, he finally met her face to face. He came dashing out of his block one Saturday afternoon to do some shopping at the local mall. At the same time, she rounded the corner, a basket of groceries on her arm, and almost knocked him to the ground.

He wasn't sure who was the most flustered or embarrassed. She'd dropped her bag and a few vegetables and packs fell on the ground. He hurriedly picked them up, re-packing her bag for her. A selection of salad stuff, root vegetables and – his heart fluttered in relief. Two supermarket packs of beef and pork, all laid on plastic dishes and covered in film. Labelled, weighed, dated. All legit. If, as appeared, she was cooking for herself, surely she wouldn't manage a human thigh too? This thought flitted through his mind as he dusted off the packs and popped them back in her bag.

"So clumsy of me, I'm sorry," he said. "Are you okay?"

"Fine, and I apologise too. I should have been looking where I was going instead of barrelling round the corner like that."

He knew this was the time to introduce himself. If he didn't do it now, he'd kick himself forever.

"My name's Paul Gunderson. I live in the block opposite yours. Same floor, actually. I've seen you cooking so I know where you live." He blushed and fluffed his lines. "I mean, that's not meant to be as threatening as it sounds!"

"I didn't take it that way, don't worry. I'm Rose. Yeah, I've looked up once or twice and seen you, but it wasn't obvious you were watching. I didn't feel I was being stalked at all." She laughed at the thought, and Paul found himself laughing too.

"Maybe we could, I don't know, get a coffee together some time? Watching you has taught me so much about cooking. I definitely owe you."

"What a lovely idea. Tell you what, you're on your way out, I'm on my way in. When you get back, stick a bit of card in your window as a signal, and I'll come down here. We can meet up and go for that coffee."

Paul flew round the shopping mall like he'd never done before. He forgot half the things he'd gone for but he didn't care. He had a date, if only for coffee, and he was a man with a mission. To get to know Rose.

As he dashed inside, he saw Dorothy standing in her open doorway, a big smile on her face. She'd seen the encounter in the street opposite and must have come to some conclusion of her own. No doubt that living alone and people-watching as much as she did, she was a great interpreter of body language. She certainly couldn't fail to see the huge smile on his face as he approached the lift. She nodded, gave him a big wink, and retreated into her own apartment.

Shoving the produce into his kitchen cupboards and refrigerator, he remembered the signal. Card, card, surely to God he had a bit of card? Eventually he grabbed a sheet of brightly coloured paper from a jotter block and stuck that in the window with clear tape. That would do. He couldn't see Rose at her kitchen window but she had more rooms, just as he did. She could be anywhere. But he knew she'd check for his signal and come out as soon as she'd seen it.

He pushed the lift button but decided he couldn't wait. Dashing down the stairs he passed the other doorways, wondering what anyone else was doing that was as exciting as his afternoon promised to be. He had to acknowledge he was a bit obsessive about Rose. Probably loneliness, he knew. Apart from Joe, he'd not really connected with anyone else in this new town. Obsession. That was something that connected him with the killer. He must shake that horrible thought.

Dorothy waved to him as he passed her window and crossed over to Rose's block. She wasn't out yet, but he knew there could be anyone watching him from those windows either side of the street. Self-consciously, he stood by her block door, waiting and trying to see if there was anyone behind those windows. Anyone other than the ever-watchful Dorothy.

He didn't have to wait long. The door swooshed outward and Rose, in a flurry of wide skirt and floral scent, ran out, almost right into him again. It didn't seem as if she went anywhere slowly.

"I hope you've not waited long?" she asked. "I looked out and saw your sign already there."

"Couple of minutes, that's all. Do you have a favourite place to go?"

They walked close together but still slightly apart toward the mall. Rose seemed to want to stand near, but not to make contact. He could feel the flesh of his arm burning as they walked with an inch or two between them. He was too shy, too inexperienced to reach for her hand. Let that come later, he thought. Rose took him to a small coffee shop that, according to her, served the best breakfast in the area. It was early evening now, but the place was still busy. They ordered coffees and found a small table near the back.

"So, how long have you lived there?" Paul asked. "I'm new to the place myself."

"Two years, nearly. I'm not a local either. I came here when my boyfriend and I split up."

"Oh, I'm sorry," Paul said, feeling absolutely no sorrow at all.

"Yeah, wasn't nice. Trouble was, we'd known each other from childhood. Our parents were friends. Our brothers and sisters played together when they were small. It was all too tangled. We couldn't have split if I'd stayed. We'd always be seeing each other. I didn't think I could bear it."

"Pity you were the one who had to move. Sounds like you've lost all that family support."

"Well, it was my decision to end it so I suppose I had to be the one to make the move. Anyway, you're new here too."

"New job, new city – no friends!"

"Ha! Well you've got one now," Rose said as she took another sip of her drink. "So, I taught you to cook, you said?"

Paul began to tell her how he'd been eating take-away food and unhealthy snacks until he'd seen her at her window preparing fresh vegetables. He wanted to tell her about the hypnotic effect of her capable hands cutting and sweeping away the finely chopped produce but thought it would sound weird. There was enough weirdness in this neighbourhood already.

"So you thought you'd copy me?" She cocked an eyebrow as she asked. He felt embarrassed to have to admit that he had.

Eventually they got onto the hot topic in the neighbourhood. "Aren't you afraid, going out early on your own?" he asked.

"I was when I first heard of it, but since I stick to the streets on my way to work, and they're fairly busy even early in the morning, I just keep my head down and make a dash for it."

"Which is how you come to knock into neighbours?" He softened the comment with a smile.

"Yep! I shop in my lunch hour a couple of times in the week. Then it's only the middle of the afternoon when I come home. I feel as safe as anyone can with a deranged killer on the loose."

"So, not very safe, then?"

A wry look was his answer.

After that first meeting – was it too small, too short, to call it a date – they met for lunch the following day. Overnight the news had broken of a fifth victim. Another innocent person butchered and within a half mile of where they lived.

"They've all been males up to now," Rose said. "It makes me feel a little safer out there."

"Do you suppose that's because, well, there's more meat on a man's leg?"

They agreed that getting into the mind of a mass killer was impossible.

Rose was so easy to talk to. He found himself telling her about his job, his hopes of friendly jaunts to the pub with workmates who turned out to be busy people with their own lives who didn't feel inclined to open up and let him in. Eventually he came around to seeing her cooking and enjoying watching her. He really hoped that didn't come over as too weird. Then he confessed that he'd though she might be cutting up human flesh for her casserole dish.

He was afraid he'd blown it. She was frozen with shock. She put down her fork and stared at the table. What could he say? How could he get out of this huge, horrible blunder?

She looked up at him and her mouth twitched slightly at the corner. "I thought you admired my cooking skills, Paul?"

"Tell you the truth I had this dream and it was you chasing me with that little chopper of yours!"

"Stopping you from running away from me?"

"Well, a slash to the hamstring will have that effect, I suppose. I've thought since that as both you and the killer were on my mind, I ran you both together. You can't be responsible for what you dream, you know."

She looked down again, for what seemed to him like a very long moment. Then her eyes met his again and that tell-tale twitch tickled both sides of her mouth. "It's not a joking matter, though, is it?" The twitch became more pronounced.

"No, it's not. It's deadly serious." He felt the humour, perhaps it was hysteria, blossoming inside him till, at the same time, they both hooted with laughter. Several fellow customers stared at them.

Rose reached out across the table and grasped his hand. He reined in his laughter and gently squeezed hers. "Thanks," he said. "I feel as if I needed permission to laugh. Things are so awful at the moment. You don't realise that the worry is dogging you all the time, even on those occasions you're not aware of it. Watching you cooking has been a relief these last few weeks. I'm so glad we bumped into each other."

"Me too."

Over the next few days, further leg bones turned up, some farther away. Each matched the DNA of one of the victims. The press were having a field day. Most thought cannibalism was the reason for the killings. A small voice of reason in one of the newscasts suggested there was no proof – but why else strip off the meat? To feed a hungry dog? No, the killings seemed more ritualistic than that. There was something about consuming the flesh of another that was supposed to transfer their powers to you, said a news anchor one night. That stirred the hornets' nest again, with many a weirdo coming out of the woodwork with magical theories.

Meanwhile, Paul and Rose grew ever closer and Dorothy's wink almost turned into a facial tic it was used so often. They began to eat together, taking turns to make the meal. It made Paul pull out all his best dishes to impress someone who was evidently a better cook than he was. Rose praised his efforts and suggested slight improvements to him, all without making him feel he'd made a dog's breakfast of their meal.

On the days he went over to her apartment he'd stand and watch her cooking. She didn't mind being scrutinised as she pulled things out of the fridge and she told him why she was doing each thing and why she'd chosen every ingredient. It didn't feel like a lesson, but he knew he was learning a lot from her.

"I'm so glad I'm the kind of inquisitive person who stares into other people's flats," he said. "Otherwise we'd not have met."

"We would, but you wouldn't have known who I was."

"Did you ever look over to my apartment and see me watching you? It could have been a bit unnerving, I suppose, though I didn't think that at the time."

"I may have glanced up a time or two, yes, but not for long enough to notice you were watching me. Not because I'm not inquisitive, just because I didn't want to add my finger to the stew."

"Eurgh," Paul said, screwing down the corners of his mouth. "Now *that* would be cannibalism."

Rose paused in her rapid chopping movements and looked up at him with a smile. Then, almost on instinct, since that had been the subject of their discussion, they looked across the road at Paul's apartment. Its blinds were adjusted slightly but, had he been there by the window, he'd have been visible.

Then, movement dragged their eyes downward. In the window of the apartment below his, someone also preparing a meal. Mike, wearing yellow rubber gloves, hefted a heavy wooden chopping board over to protect his work surface. Then he brought a joint of meat over to it, presumably from his out-of-sight fridge. He lifted a powerful butcher's cleaver and brought it down onto the joint, cutting off a good sized steak.

Rose dropped her chopper, leaned over the sink and vomited. Paul put his hand on her back for connection and comfort for both of them.

He watched in horrid fascination as Mike returned the joint out of sight.

"That was a human femur."

The Easter Riots

The Easter Chickens were up in arms. Well, wings would be more accurate. "It has come to my notice," said Chocky, the shop steward of the Easter Chickens' Union, "that there has recently been a flood of chocolate bunnies getting in on the act. I think we should take this to Eostre, the goddess of spring, and our patron. She's the boss, so she can decide."

She was encouraged by a chorus of "Chook, chook," "Bok, bok," and "Bwerk!" from the assembled chickens.

"Everyone ready to go?" she asked, and had to wait while one or two of the assembled chocolate egg-laying hens popped one out before they were ready to waddle off in search of a higher authority. Such an argument over job demarcation had never before existed in the Land of Myths and Legends.

They ambled, waddled and pecked their way into the sacred glade of Eostre, where the goddess sat upon her green throne in robes of chartreuse and yellow, the embodiment of the return of the spring.

"My lady," began Chocky, "we would like your ruling on a matter of our job's terms and conditions."

Great Eostre rose gracefully to her feet, her bare toes adorned with a tasteful scatter of primrose petals. The same flowers, and many-hued crocus blossoms, garlanded her hair.

"Speak, little layer-of-eggs," she said.

"Madam, we have always understood our role to be the provision of chocolate Easter Eggs for the children of the world."

"And so it is," replied the great one.

"So how come there's this so-called 'Easter Bunny' character muscling in on our territory?" The rest of the flock, pushing and shoving, and occasionally pecking the sacred grass, joined in with "Yeah," "Too right," "What she said," and still the occasional "Bwerk!"

"He is also a herald of spring," replied the lady. "It is his place as much as yours to bring in the season."

It was all Chocky could do to calm the riot of clucking. "Sisters!" she clucked. "Please, calm yourselves. Let us reason with the great one."

Calm eventually descended, with a flurry of feathers and the odd accidental mini egg. "Our argument is, Your Ladyship, that… like… since when do rabbits lay eggs eh? Answer me that."

Eostre blinked once, slowly. "I see. Well, of course they don't do they? They produce baby rabbits. Rather a lot of them. But the Easter Bunny is a tradition. Children love to receive chocolate bunnies, just as they love your chocolate eggs."

More clucking, more flying feathers. "But it's not right that they should get the credit for our eggs!"

More riotous assembly from the flock. "Nah, what's eggs got to do with them, eh?" cried one.

An old dear from the back sqwawked, "That's cultural appropriation, that is!"

Eostre looked down upon the panicking flock. A couple of primrose petals drifted from her chaplet. Her usually benign expression clouded slightly. "Hear me, oh Easter Chickens. Of course the bunnies can't bring the eggs. Only you can do

31

that." There was much satisfied clucking from the assembly. "But the children receive your Easter eggs, and also, sometimes, chocolate bunnies to eat."

"Oh, well, that's different, innit?" said a hen from the back. "As long as they're eating him but not us, that's okay."

"Yeah, so long as we get the credit."

"Eating chocolate rabbits is fine by us," said Chocky. "And we give our eggs freely. Just so long as people aren't eating chickens."

A chorus of, "Too right," and "Yeah!" followed.

"Imagine humans eating chickens," sniggered Chocky.

Eostre's gentle smile froze slightly. She bestowed upon them her most tender look. Adjusting her now slightly wonky chaplet of spring flowers and carefully tucking her green and yellow robes beneath her, she resumed her place on the green throne.

The hens pottered about, pecking at the grass and wandering off in all directions, their sense of purpose now dissipated.

Chocky bowed before the throne. "Come on, girls," she called to her wayward flock. "Back home to do the duty!" Now they had no firm purpose in view, the hens wandered aimlessly and were soon spread throughout the spring landscape. Chocky rapidly discovered that chickens are easily satisfied, and there are harder things to herd than cats.

Arbow's Notebook

You could say this is my diary although I have never written in it.

I fell in with a man of science by the name of David Arbow. We were both acolytes of John Dee's, a man who straddled the boundary between science and magic. These days he is thought of as a magician and an occultist although when we first knew him he was concerned with communicating with angels. It was through this cabalistic angel magic and his beliefs that man has the capability of divine power that David Arbow came under his influence.

Contrary to common belief, Dee was a devout Christian and a gifted mathematician and his reputation for black magic is not founded in reality. Arbow, however, loved the idea of communicating with angels, most particularly with those angels who fell, along with Lucifer, when challenging the Divine One for power. He felt that if he could speak to these entities, steal a little of the power they surely possessed, he himself would rise above his fellow men. His arrogance refused to let him consider anything else.

He had nowhere near the calibre of mind which his hero possessed. He would sit with Dee while the latter performed calculations, nodding and seemingly sharing the journey of learning with him, but he was floundering along the wayside.

Without the Master he was lost. Nevertheless, he had accumulated a certain cachet amongst Dee's other hangers-on and sought to reap financial rewards through this reputation.

We were all in awe of John Dee's mind and the things of which he was capable. Most of us were content to study with him and in all honesty, we struggled to follow in his wake, let alone keep up with him. Those of a more esoteric frame of mind would try to emulate his far-seeing techniques and attempt to contact spirits and even angelic beings by use of an Aztec artefact – an obsidian scrying mirror.

Doctor Dee would occasionally allow those of us of lesser talents to attempt to see with this device but I have to confess, I saw nothing. Arbow let it be known that he could contact heavenly beings and also lost souls, adrift in a void and looking for the way into celestial bliss. Dee was interested and gave Arbow special attention, though the rest of us believed he was being fooled by a cunning man of lesser talents.

Dee encouraged Arbow to make copious notes in a diary. He suggested he should note the days on which he made the contacts, the results of his 'conversations' with the angelic forms and even the weather conditions prevalent at the time. He told Arbow that the diary must be a special book and that it should never be used for anything else. It was the key to heaven.

It was to me. It is made from my skin.

Six on the Beach

Yes. I'm embarrassed and ashamed to admit that I thought that's what the cocktail was called. Dom and I went backpacking for a few months straight after graduating. We had a ball in Australia and this gorgeous hunk of a barman with the thickest Aussie accent you could imagine told me I'd like this cocktail. He made it for me several times and I could have sworn he said 'six'. It was ages before I knew it was Sex on the Beach, and boy, did I feel stupid. I'd convinced myself it was the six ingredients (if you counted the ice) that gave it the name. Live and learn (and blush) as they say.

I also felt totally stupid when I asked Dom why the barman always called me Ned. I'm only glad I didn't ask the hunk himself. "It's cos your name is Kelly, love."

"And…?" Blank.

"Ned Kelly? Aussie outlaw? You know, all the stories about him?"

Well obviously I didn't know or I'd not have embarrassed myself by asking. I can't believe how naïve I was back then. It all died down, of course, when we returned to rainy Britain, found jobs, got a mortgage and, a few years down the line, had our first child, Ben. We were both the only child in our families so we wanted a good handful of our own. Davie and Alice followed in short order and we thought that was it. A few years after Alice, Joe popped out. Almost literally by then. It was one thing I was really good at – popping out babies. Four was enough, I thought. When we had our first seaside jaunt with all the children, I was almost tempted to go for number five when Dom resurrected the Six on the Beach joke. He thought it was a joke. My smile was sort of riveted in place.

When baby Joe was two and a bit and a fierce little toddler, we took a cottage for a week at the seaside. We'd done the same before he was born so we knew the children would just enjoy pottering on the sand, foraging in the rock pools and eating sandy sandwiches – all the things children have done for generations.

On the first day we carried a rug, a basket of supplies, a book for Dom and a magazine for me, and the children carried their buckets and spades. We were really blessed with the weather. It was late June and we wangled the older ones a week off school so we could afford it.

Dom and I set up base camp in a little inlet between the rocks. The coastline formed miniature bays and they made popular places for families to park themselves as the inlets acted as a windbreak. Dom began by scraping the sand into a sort of sofa shape before throwing the rug over it. He was a past master at sand sculpture and it was certainly a bit more comfortable than lying flat out.

Before I allowed any beach-based shenanigans I made the children line up so I could slather them in sun block. The result was always a slippery, sticky child but at least there would be no sunburn and no tears at bedtime. Not for that reason, anyway. A sticky child, of course, is one who attracts the sand and I knew that before we could leave the beach, dusting them clean enough to slip on their outer clothes would be a nightmare. Unless I could sluice them down with rock-pool water, which was likely to be a little warmer than the sea. Let's be honest, the ice cubes in the G&T that I'd promised myself this evening would be warmer than the North Sea, even in summer.

The youngsters, duly processed to deter the sun, began by filling their buckets with whatever caught their eyes. With Ben it was always bits of seaweed. I remember the first seaside holiday we had with him, when Davie was a babe in arms and Alice and Joe not thought of. As we packed to go home he sneaked his favourite strands of seaweed into a side pocket in Dom's rucksack. It was several weeks later when we found where the horrible smell was coming from.

Alice always found delightful pieces of rock she couldn't live without. If Dom and I bred a geologist, it would be Alice. This time, true to form, she headed for the banks of pebbles that licked up along the shore from the tide line. "Are you allowed just to take stones off the beach?" I asked Dom. "Don't you need a licence to abstract minerals, or something?"

"I've no idea. But what happens the day before we go home? We always persuade her to keep just a couple of special ones and I end up fetching the rest back. You probably need a licence to dump minerals too. Still, I'm not going to lose any sleep, or any reading time, over it."

Davie had always contented himself with simply shovelling sand. He was the structural engineer of the family.

After half an hour or so of pottering they scooted off down the beach to where the sand was damp, the better to get their constructions under way. "Don't wander off," Dom yelled.

A desultory chorus of muttering greeted that reasonable request and, after watching them fondly for a few moments, we settled to read. Bliss. Reading in the sun, in the warmth, in the very gentle breeze. It should always be like this. Dom settled to his paperback. I flicked and scanned through the magazine I'd bought at the shop on the promenade. There were one or two interesting articles but they were scattered with total trivia, to my mind.

"Listen to this," I proclaimed.

Dom propped his book on his knee for a moment.

"Page 15 is 'How to achieve a beach-ready body in two weeks.' Damn all use that is when we're already on holiday. And the facing page says 'Upgrade your afternoon teas with our fool-proof Victoria sponge' – honestly. How do you get a beach-ready body if you're continually stuffing Vicky sponge in your pie-hole?"

Dom leaned back and gave me that slightly aloof smile he gives the children when they do anything clever. As though he got the point, but wasn't sufficiently persuaded to actually agree with me. He put his head back in his book and mumbled, "Seals have a beach-ready body all the time. I don't suppose they have to make any effort."

For a moment I was gobstruck. Was he really comparing me to a seal? Actually, I thought, there's the barrel-shaped body, like a fat cigar. The lack of a waist. Hmm. Maybe. But by the time I'd worked out that it wasn't what any woman wanted even to have hinted at, the moment had gone and unless I truly wanted to drag him out of his book and into an almighty row, I should leave it alone. Except by rigorous starvation, it didn't seem possible to get back to the slender form of my backpacking days with four children under my belt. So to speak.

In a spirit of enquiry, I lifted the loose top I was wearing. Bikini days were long past and I now approached a beach holiday with midi shorts and a sloppy top. No point in showing off my inadequacies to the world. 'A wise man sits on the hole in his carpet,' as the old saying has it. The scene I discerned was like a contour map. Silver traceries of rivers between the plateaux showed the stretch marks that were the battle scars of motherhood. In spite of smug magazine writers, I hadn't found any magic formula for deterring or banishing those shiny marks. No fantastically expensive unguent, however frequently applied, could alter the fact that your skin was pulled wide enough to house two people, even if one of them was a very small one. And after the birth – well, you can bolt your stable door all you like, but the horse has made its break for freedom.

How hard can it be to get back into shape, I wondered. Still gazing at my navel and its vast surroundings, I clenched my stomach muscles. The flesh bunched up most unevenly and unattractively into mounds and bumps. It looked like porridge in the microwave, bubbling away for just those few seconds before it goes volcanic and coats the inside of the oven. My erstwhile waist land was now a wasteland.

I dragged myself from such self-pitying musing to cast an eye over the construction site between our camp and the gradually encroaching tide. The little workmen had created quite an edifice, with mottes and baileys, battlements and berms. Ben couldn't see a top without going over it. He was the organiser and could spend the whole of such a game waving his spade and giving orders. Davie would be the one doing all the earth moving. He had great spatial awareness and could make things with his Lego that were beyond the imagination of his older brother. Things with wheels and motors, where Ben was still building walls. But Ben played to his strengths too. He'd even managed to divest Alice of some of her precious stones to decorate the castellations. As I admired it, I subconsciously counted – to three.

"Where's Joe?" I asked, frowning now.

The three of them looked up and shrugged. Well, Ben and Alice shrugged. Davie looked up as though nothing impinged upon his world of sand. I doubt he could even have repeated the question.

"Joe? Joey!" I called. I was now seriously worried. My

youngest, my baby, was missing. The others didn't know where he was. They didn't remember him wandering away. I so much wanted to shake Ben and ask how he could have let it happen, but it wasn't Ben's fault. It was mine. I should have been watching my little boy instead of feeling inadequate and inspecting my bloody stretch marks.

Dom had put his arm around me now, as I felt myself begin to shake. "Look, I'll go that way, you go the other," he said. "He could be anywhere. He could just be behind that little rock."

"He's so small, Dom. What if he's fallen and hurt himself? He's such an attractive child. Someone could have snatched him." Hot tears were scalding my eyes now and I thought I might faint.

Dom gave my shoulders a squeeze. "Don't lose it in front of the other kids, Kel. Not just yet. Let's have a thorough search."

"You three, stay right where you are!" I yelled and, apparently unconcerned about their missing sibling, they returned to their excavations. "I don't want to lose another one." As I said the words, I felt my throat begin to close and the heat of unshed tears stung my eyes.

After giving me a quick kiss, Dom turned and began walking south, close to the low cliff so he could inspect every little curve and cranny. Let's hope he'd quickly find a little boy so absorbed in his game that he didn't realise he was playing alone. I dragged my eyes from him and walked in the other direction, praying that we didn't have to leave as five on the beach.

I scrambled over some boulders and into the next little bay, calling out Joe's name as I went. I was in a panic and could feel my heart like a lump of lead in my chest. Slipping, I grazed my knuckles on a barnacle and swore under my breath. Where was he? Had someone really taken him?

Then I saw it. Joe's sun hat was plonked on the sand. He loved that hat and wouldn't part with it willingly. I was sure now that someone had kidnapped our youngest. Images of him screaming and wriggling – wouldn't we have heard? – gave way to thoughts of a cloth soaked in chloroform held tightly over his little face. Even to myself I sounded like a Victorian melodrama – but what else was the explanation? I was hyperventilating now but couldn't get sufficient grip on myself to slow my breathing down. My vision was closing in and I thought I was going to faint.

Dom had heard me shriek when I saw the sun hat. He dashed up behind me, overtook me, and snatched it up off the hot sand.

"S'prise!" Joey's moon-faced smile beamed up at us from under the hat. Behind us we could hear the giggles from the other three, maybe feeling a bit guilty now, seeing how much upset it had caused. With a seismic eruption, little fat toes, chubby knees and arms, wriggled their way out of the sand and Joe jumped up into my arms for a cuddle. He was giggling uncontrollably. To him – and to the others – it was just a great laugh.

After sobbing with relief for several minutes, I was brewing up a head of anger and looking for someone to slap. "Dominic Evans, you taught them to do this. Last year, you showed them how to bury their dad in the sand, just your face showing. You gave them the idea. I can't really blame them."

"Oh, come on, Kel. Everyone buries their dad. It's part of childhood beach holidays. I bet you buried yours?" I had, true enough. "And it's we dads who encourage it. Who shows children how to bury Dad in the sand? The dad, that's who. It's a rite of passage, being allowed to bury a parent in the sand."

"Stop being so bloody calm and logical about it. I really

41

thought we'd lost one of our children. And there I was worrying about beach bodies and stretch marks – and we could have lost our baby!"

"We didn't though, did we? Come on, buck up," he said. "Fetch some water in your bucket, Ben, and let's get everyone clean, dried and dressed."

Ben complied and with much complaining about the sand stinging as I rubbed each precious body with extra vigour, they were finally ready to face the town. I'd had enough of the beach for the day.

"These kids are starving," Dom said. "Let's see if we can turn Six on the Beach to Six go for Fish and Chips." The children looked puzzled initially. Six on the beach wasn't a term they'd understand. But everyone understood fish and chips! The smiles said it all.

Hit and Run

Billy was on his winding way home from the pub when it happened. That was his excuse for what he did later. He lived beyond the adopted road, down the gravelled track where the street-lights didn't reach, but before he got that far, his ears were assaulted by a screeching of brakes. He leapt back, fearful for his life, as he heard a thud, smelled burning rubber, and an old van roared past him, its wheels screaming as it turned and disappeared back down the road.

As Billy watched it, he saw a dark shadow under a clipped yew hedge. A crumpled bag of rags, by the look of it. Heart still hammering in his chest, he approached it. Might be something there worth having. On his miserable wage in his grim little cottage, he wasn't too proud to take old clothes he found. They'd wash. There was often a lot of wear in the stuff the posh people chucked out.

He staggered over to take a good look. He almost fell over when he saw the clothes contained a body. Or more accurately, the wreck of a body. Instinctively, Billy knelt and touched his fingers to the neck of the most lovely girl he'd ever seen. Not that he saw that many. They avoided him. Went the other way, sat at a different table. This girl was beautiful. Her face was, at any rate.

Her legs were splayed at such bizarre angles they must

have been broken in several places. High, impossibly high heeled shoes had fallen from her feet. Her torso seemed to have been crushed, and there was blood, so much blood coming from so many places that the smart clothes she'd worn were now in ruins. Her right arm was thrown back away from her body, again, broken. Her left was curled almost protectively over her chest. Too late to protect her.

He knew he should get help, as he'd felt the tiny flutter of life still at her throat. He should report it to the ambulance service and the police. It was a hit-and-run and that was not right. He dragged his ancient phone from his trouser pocket and pressed 999. Sitting back on his heels, he told the call handler what he'd heard, and the state the body was in. He was asked to stay with the girl and wait, as the paramedics would be there very soon. As he watched, describing the wounds, the fragile remains of life left her, and her lovely face drained of colour. She was so very pale.

The sirens grew louder as the ambulance approached. Billy didn't want to stay. It was all too sad. He didn't want the police to interview him either. He could do no more for the tragic victim. Just as he was about to get unsteadily to his feet, he noticed the glint of the streetlight on her left hand. The most beautiful engagement ring winked at him. It was huge. If those stones were real, the ring was probably worth half the value of his hovel of a cottage. That poor girl. She didn't need it now. He slipped it off her cooling hand and into his pocket.

Billy made his escape down the unlit lane to his home and, after all the excitement, not to mention the pints of beer, he threw himself onto his scruffy bed and entered oblivion.

He woke with a groan the next morning. It was early – he was used to early rising for his groundsman job at the local big house. The pittance of a wage was supposed to be offset by the tied cottage. It was just a trap. He dragged himself out of bed then stopped short as the previous night swam into focus. As he went through his vestigial ablutions and made an instant coffee and a slice of toast, he remembered the hit-and-run. He remembered the beauty of the victim – then he remembered the ring.

Fishing about in his noisome pocket, he felt the chilly metal, the bumpy feel of the stones. In the cold light of morning, in the squalor of his dark little cottage, it shone like a beacon of hope. Those two diamonds were enormous. And the red stone they flanked – surely that was a ruby. A bluish-pink ruby – not a dark red chip of something. A massive, gorgeous, edible-looking sweetie of a stone. His memory of last night, of thinking it was worth half his cottage, was overthrown by the realisation it was worth far more.

Selling it would be the difficulty. Maybe he'd need to wait – a year or more, even – and go to another town – but someone would give him good money for this. A lot of very good money.

It was a week or more before he could once more face going down that lane that led to his little gravel track. The memory of his helplessness in the face of death came back to him. He crossed the great park and took his evening refreshment in a different pub for a few nights.

Eventually he decided to go back to his old haunt. They knew him there. Nobody took any notice of him, though he stood out like a mourner at a wedding in the posher pub. He was part of the fittings at his usual place. After an evening of consuming a meat pie followed by sinking several pints, he set off for home. As he got to the end of the lane where the accident had happened, he felt unaccountably nervous. He told himself not to be so stupid. It was Halloween and the old kids' stories had got to him.

He pulled his shoulders back and walked towards home once again. A cat on a garden wall took one look at him and screeched, arching its back. Hissing, it jumped down into the garden and streaked away. He shrugged and continued.

What was that sound?

Billy turned around, feeling suddenly cold, and swept the lane with his eyes. Nobody there. A second time, he jumped and turned. It sounded like the click of high heels on a pavement. Someone was messing with him, ducking down behind the garden gates whenever he turned.

He reached the place where the accident had happened. The shadows seemed to thicken here – but it was under a big hedge. Nothing surprising in that. He admitted to his fear, though, and crossed the road to walk on the other side. Another slight noise, on the edge of hearing, and again he looked behind him. That sounded like a deep sigh. But how could it be? There was nobody there. And why should he worry? He wasn't responsible for the death. He'd only… well, yes, he'd robbed a corpse, technically. But that wasn't as bad, was it? Not as bad as killing a young woman (who wore those clicking high heels) and stealing her future. If she were haunting Billy now, what on earth was she doing to her killer? He wouldn't like to be in that person's shoes tonight.

He passed the dark space, trying to keep his face to it, yet still he could hear footsteps, and deep sighing, just behind him. This was ridiculous. Despite his terrible diet he was a fairly fit man, he thought. He turned to face his own little roadway, hidden in the dark as it was. He began to sprint, but he couldn't get away from the sounds – couldn't see anyone behind him as he turned, twisted, whirled through three hundred and sixty degrees in a panic as he tried to see who was making them.

Soon it was hard to tell which were his follower's hollow breaths and which his own desperate gasps. He threw himself forward into the all-enveloping darkness of the little track just as the moon cleared the clouds. The footsteps behind him stopped, and the little laugh brought the hairs on his neck upright. She was so near, now. He must be able to see her.

Again, he whirled round, but there was nobody there. Only his shadow.

Two shadows.

They found his body the next morning when he didn't show up for work. Heart attack, the doctor said. No wonder, with his unhealthy lifestyle, they all said in the pub. Strange, though, that he stayed in that horrid little cottage when he had such a valuable ring in his kitchen drawer.

Spring Flowers

I'm really enjoying this. Here on my kneeler, trowel in hand, weeding between my newly flowering spring bulbs. I've always loved bulbs, all flowers really, but Carl wouldn't let me grow them. He wouldn't let me do a lot of things, now I think about it. How did he stop me? I've lost count of the number of times I've been to A&E having 'fallen down the stairs' or 'bumped into a door'. He always said he hated gardens and gardening, and I was so useless that anything I started would fail and he'd have to sort it out. Lazy bastard.

This is the first project I've taken on by myself since we married, eight years ago. It wasn't easy. This had been compacted lawn. That's all we had in the garden, grass. Things are going to change now.

He disappeared in the autumn last year. Naturally I reported him missing, but he's a grown man, and his passport and a few bits of clothing had gone too. As the officer who responded to my call said, it wasn't a police matter if he chose to leave by himself. As an adult, he was presumably in no danger and it was up to him where he went. So I've managed fine by myself since then. The deserted wife, but not totally useless, eh, Carl? I'm not the first wife to be abandoned and I won't be the last.

I was in a garden centre last autumn for the first time in

years when I saw a big stand of bulbs. Lots of large and miniature daffodils, a few species tulips, spring squills, grape hyacinths, crocuses, all sorts of things. As he wasn't there to stop me, I squandered most of that week's housekeeping money on packets of wizened looking corms and plump little bulbs. It was worth it, even though I lived on mashed potatoes for a week. Some are in flower now, some will give me a succession of colour. It just lifts the soul to stand with my morning coffee and look at them from the kitchen window. Glorious. Carl doesn't know what he's missing.

I really wondered if I'd taken on too much when I began the digging. The ground was so hard and dry, but as I persisted, the rain began to fall and soaked the dry earth, making my task easier. I had to dig deep. Bulbs need planting at a reasonable depth if they aren't to come up 'blind' eventually – nothing but leaves. So I persisted. It took me most of a day and a night to do the job, but I was determined.

Down and down I dug, making sure my new treasures would have room for deep roots. The advantage of well-planted spring bulbs is they're with you every year, bringing colour, beauty and hope.

I've put away my trowel and kneeler now, scrubbed up my hands and made a coffee. I'll spend the next few minutes enjoying the fruits of my labour. Then it'll be time to get ready for work. Yes, I now have a part time job. Just a bit of shop work but I've never had that since I married Carl. It's a start and I'm looking for something I can actually live on, a career like I had before marriage. Since then, I've never had my own money to spend as I like. Things are tight, but I'm happy again, as I never thought I'd be.

I think I got the gardening bug from my dad. They live so far away now but I've begun seeing them again – Christmas was fantastic. He's encouraging me to dig a bit more and start a vegetable plot. After this success, I think I might. He always uses bone-meal on his garden, but just on the vegetable patch, I think.

I wonder if it's good for bulbs? I wonder if it works with whole bones?

We'll see.

The Tree

This tree has come to symbolise my life.

I was nineteen years old and taking part in early experiments in electrical conductivity when something happened that made me different from others. I believe it occurred when one of our experiments went badly wrong. We were passing a powerful current through a cadaver and I caught the full blast in error. I was thrown across the laboratory and had my hair singed. I even lost consciousness for a time and spent two days in hospital recovering.

It was after this that I realised, very gradually, that physical changes which affected my fellows left me untouched. I didn't age. Oh, I don't mean I still look nineteen. I have filled out a little and my facial features have matured. That was all over a hundred and fifty years ago though. Unless someone cuts off my head, shoots me or runs me through with a blade, I will live on, potentially forever.

So many people think that it must be wonderful never to age - never to die. They don't know what they're talking about. Being immortal doesn't stop you from falling in love. Every woman I have ever loved has aged before my eyes, has become bent, grey and wrinkled. She has died of sickness or old age and I have lost her. It happens to many people once. It has happened to me several times, that I have buried the

51

woman I love while appearing to the outside world as though I were her grandson.

When I lost Lilian, my first wife, I buried her and planted a seed above her withered body. The tree that grew there would be her remembrance. I go back every year and watch as it grows. It's in the prime of life but I have buried three other beloved women since its seed was sown. I now know that I will either live alone and desolate, or I will love women yet unborn and lose them too. It's not just the loss that hurts, it's watching helplessly as day by day she slips away from me. I am now aware that my memory tree has reached its own maturity and will begin to decline. I shall have to collect seeds from it and begin another tree.

Now my fifth wife is white-haired and looks like my grandmother. For the first time, with this wife, Ellen, I have a son. After a wonderful childhood I watched him grow, taught him much and now see him looking like my father. My life feels like a tragedy.

Today is the anniversary of Lilian's death and my first great grief. I stand under the canopy of my mourning tree and finger the seed in my pocket. Unless I take my own life, I will need another tree to commemorate my lost loves - and children.

I stoop, bury the seed in the damp earth and stand back.

The Summer of 'Twenty-two

The wife's doing me head in. Things weren't so bad when we were both working and only had to tolerate each other for the evenings. I think the rot set in when the kids grew up and left home. Then she only had me to nag and micro-manage and it's a bit much when you're an adult. The idyllic retirement went down the pan pretty sharpish. She doesn't really have many hobbies, just gossiping with her cronies at a supposed book group, though she rarely reads the book in time for the meetings. They took a break in the worst of the pandemic, of course, but they're back again now.

No, her hobby, it seems, is interfering with mine. I thought when I retired I'd be able to pick up the things I loved but hadn't had time to do. I used to love restoring old motorbikes before we married.

"Where do you think you're going to put that?"

"I can work on it in the garage, love."

"And where's the car going to go?"

"It'll be fine on the drive."

"We didn't pay good money to keep a car on the drive so it can rust away in the rain. And don't think you're bringing that oily mess into the kitchen!"

See what I mean? And my other hobby was jigsaws. I do love a jigsaw. I had some really good ones, thousands of pieces, but she gave them away without a by-your-leave. No point arguing. When I started them it was, "You'll have to shift that. I want to set the table." I got a big board to do them on, so I could move the whole thing at mealtimes, but no, that wasn't good enough. "It makes the place look scruffy, Bill."

The latest is the last straw. She went to some talk at the WI about 'edible flowers'. Seems a shame to pull their heads off for a salad when they don't even taste of anything. She said it's no different from cutting flowers for a vase. I disagree. You can still admire their beauty in a vase.

Anyway, nothing would do but we had to go to a garden centre and buy her latest fad. Nasturtiums, pansies, English marigolds, borage and day-lilies. Day-lilies? I'd never heard of them and I know she hadn't. She's never done a hand's turn in the garden since we moved here, forty years ago. She doesn't know a daisy from a buttercup. She had a fad for growing vegetables a few years back, which meant that she declared we'd grow our own, but it was me that had to do it. I didn't mind. I'd have done that years ago if she hadn't told me we had to have lawn and flowerbeds because vegetables looked untidy. I quite like cultivating my little plot. It gets me away from her for a bit, anyway. But since this WI thing, I'm getting my marching orders.

We took a trip to the garden centre, filled up a trolley with the required plants and brought them home. Sandra, the total garden novice, told me where they all had to go. As usual, I ignored her and followed the instructions on the labels. Some liked the full sun, some preferred shade. She'd never notice. She wouldn't come out and look at them. Some went into flower beds and some into tubs.

As the season progressed, they came into flower and actually looked quite nice, each in its own way.

She'd occasionally give me a shout, while she was preparing a salad, to say, "Bill, fetch me some of those edible flowers, will you?" and I was dispatched out into the garden to pick them. The day-lilies, marigolds and nasturtiums were dismembered, pulled into individual petals, to scatter across her creations. I mentioned that my dad used to put a few nasturtium leaves into a salad sandwich but no, it had to be pretty, not just green. Pansy and borage flowers went in whole. Couldn't taste a thing.

The final insult came when she decided to invite the book group friends to lunch. 'Here we go,' I thought. 'Showing off again.' And sure enough, it was quiche and salad and, "Bill!" She might as well have yelled 'Stop what you're doing at once!' "Get me some salad flowers, will you?"

I came in with a slack handful of the required blooms, to be told, "And you'll have to make yourself scarce. It's all going to be book talk and I don't want you hanging around with your long face and spoiling it."

"What about my lunch?" I asked. "Don't I get any? I grew the bloody things for you!"

"No need for that attitude! I'll put some in the fridge for you to eat later. Clear off into the garden for a couple of hours, will you?" So there it was. Banned from my own dining room.

Happy to be away from the harpy, I busied myself in the greenhouse and the flower beds, till I decided to nip into the kitchen for a glass of water. I hadn't even had a drink since breakfast. I quietly ran the tap and filled my glass with cold water, when I heard her unmistakeable voice above the others. "Of course, I love growing the edible flowers for a salad. So pretty!"

"They look lovely, Sandra," said one.

"You're so talented," cried another.

'Talented my arse,' I thought. 'She can't grow them, she can't identify them, she has me to do both of those, and I don't even get a bloody lunch out of it!'

That was it. I grabbed my laptop and did a bit of research. Next time she was out with her cronies, I drove back to the garden centre and filled my trolley with towering delphiniums, monkshood, foxgloves, lily-of-the-valley, and I even splashed out on a shrub, Nerium oleander, for its lovely pink flowers. Pink has always been her favourite colour. Bringing them home, I got to work in the flower beds and by the time she came home again they blended in beautifully. Not that she'd notice.

I'd had enough. I withdrew a chunk of my hard-earned savings and booked a couple of months in a small apartment somewhere far away. I was due a bit of relief from the constant nagging, not to say bullying, I got every day. I had my eye on a motorbike to do up. It'd give me months of pleasure, then I could ride it. Just what I'd always dreamed of, but I'd come to realise that my dreams had been trampled for years under a pair of size five shoes.

I'm here now, in a ground floor flat with enough outdoor space to work on my motorbike. She'll never find me in this small Midlands town. I have the freedom and happiness I thought I'd be getting in my retirement. Lord knows what Sandra's doing and I don't even care. I left no note. I left her plenty in the bank account and a garden full of glorious flowers. What she does with them, if anything, is her call.

No doubt I'll go back in a few months' time to see how she's getting on – if I think I can face it all again. Meanwhile, bon appetite, my little dragon!

We All Fall Down

It started with a sneeze.

Someone, somewhere, caught a virus which had crossed the species boundary. Its beginning was mysterious and its spread was insidious.

This virus had come from a pig farm on the other side of the world. It only needed a couple of infected workers to board an airliner and everyone on the flight caught it. By the time people began going to the doctor's or to hospital the virus had too deep a hold to be halted. Senior Medical Officers were on the alert but the only sign that something was amiss was the sight of staff at ports and airports wearing face masks. We'd all seen that before though with scares like bird flu and SARS and they'd been false alarms. Once people began to be admitted to hospital there was little that could be done.

Stockpiled Tamiflu was brought out and given to medical staff because they were in the front line. Soon there were very few health practitioners unaffected. At this later stage anyone who wanted it was issued with the medication. It didn't halt the spread of the disease though. It couldn't cure the violent sneezing, the lung-tearing coughing fits and the raging fever which finally killed sufferers. What the medication did was upset the virus. It still killed sufferers; it just took longer to do it.

In hospitals and labs, hell, even in kitchens and bathrooms, people were trying to find something that would halt the disease. Old wives' remedies were considered on the same footing as complex formulae made up in a lab. Maybe aspirin or high doses of vitamin C might save the world. What a futile search. But we had to do something.

No one could dismiss this as another false alarm, another non-event bird flu. When people began dying in greater numbers the grave diggers and crematorium staff were working overtime. Eventually there were more corpses than there were people to bury them. We could no longer treat the bodies of neighbours and friends with respect; we had to heap them into funeral pyres. You have no idea how much fuel it takes to burn a human body. I had to do this for my own husband. I never heard what happened to my children and small grandchildren but I knew what the odds were.

Eventually, in a village of seven hundred people, only three of us remained alive; Sally, a 34 year old nurse, Joel, a 12 year old and myself. We knew early on that Sally must have an immunity to the virus, as she came into contact with so many stricken people. I still have no idea why young Joel and I were immune. We walked into the nearby town and found a similar situation. Very few people were still alive. In some places they had been burning the bodies but in other areas there were festering heaps of unattended corpses with all the additional health risk that posed. These places were soon abandoned.

The few people I was able to speak to said they had feared rioting and streets running with blood. There were too few of us for that. Sally, Joel and I decided to move into a farmhouse at the end of the village. It had a paddock we could grow vegetables in, a couple of cows we could milk and a small flock of poultry. I took on food production and cooking and

Sal, as a medic, was in demand in the town too, though she wouldn't move there. She found a bicycle in one of the sheds and would cycle in a couple of times a week. We broke into houses to raid pantries for tinned food. There was no fresh food and of course freezers stopped working and their contents stank after the power failed. Too few people with the right skills were left and water and sewerage systems failed too. Our lives became primitive. We had no idea what was happening a hundred miles away, let alone anywhere else in the world.

There were too few of us and no future. Not unless we grabbed that future with both hands. This was the point at which we could die out as a race. We had become hardened to loss after those dreadful, terrifying months when our loved ones died and we had to drag out their bodies to burn them. After you've done that, there's nothing too awful to contemplate. Our only future lay in procreation - and fast.

As was the case in our village, we found the few dozen people still alive in the town were predominantly women. For some reason the men were less likely to have a natural immunity. This meant that there was little chance of people selecting a partner in the usual way. To have a realistic chance of survival as a species we needed as many babies as we could produce. In effect, they were just another crop.

We were offered a man from the town, but in order to have his services we had to take on another three women, Lou, Ellen and Ali. I blessed the fact that my reproductive years were behind me. This was a loveless way to attempt to replace those we had lost. Ben was in his mid-forties and on the whole, seemed a decent enough man. The girls all chose a house of their own down the lane and Ben took turns staying at a different house each night. Ali fell pregnant within weeks but we had a meeting in the farmhouse kitchen where we took our meals together, and found that the girls all felt the system was disruptive. They suggested a week each. No one found the sharing satisfactory. At least, none of the girls did. I didn't hear Ben complaining!

To me he was a godsend. He was a builder by trade and had the strength and stamina that I lacked, though the active outdoor life was gradually building mine up too. One important duty that he took on was to dig a latrine pit, and erect a little shed over it. Without a sewerage system we had to go back to the old ways. Regularly he would fill it in and move the shed along by a few yards. As Joel grew stronger, he helped.

Ben also worked the land with me and was brilliant at clearing ground at planting time. Generally they defer to me in our choice of crops to grow. We had the benefit of the farm's greenhouse and as I'd always saved seeds and grown old varieties of peas and beans which we could dry, I was able to build up stocks for winter.

As time has passed, Ben and I have become very close. Although I'm a good few years older than he is, he hasn't got the pressure to perform as he has with his harem, as he calls them. Regularly, when he's 'done his duty' and the girls are all, or mostly, pregnant, he will spend the night with me. Our physical relationship is a comfort to us both. This world we're creating is built upon the foundations of horror, tragedy and deep, deep sadness. Another warm body and a person who understands, who has also loved and lost, is a great consolation. It helps so much to share hopes and fears and to keep the darkness at bay for each other.

The same situation as ours pertained in town. Little communes of three or four women to one man ensured a continuing group of pregnant women. Sally was one of them, even though she would be midwife to all the others. Each group was autonomous. We decided who would cook - in our group we took turns. Ben and Joel joined in. It was a skill everyone needed, although we ate rather a lot of egg and chips when Joel cooked. It was a challenge to widen his repertoire. I still mainly raised the vegetables and Joel helped me with a small wheat crop. He said it was the only way he would ever get a chip butty.

That was seven years ago. My life and my world are wildly different from those I had before the virus. Our village now has a small group of youngsters who we hope are immune, as their parents are. Joel is now one of our valuable men and has Amy and Lily, a couple of girls from town, as his harem. They were in their early teens when the virus struck and are now a great help with our blossoming farm. Amy is already pregnant. Lou runs the crèche. She lost three of her own babes in the year of the virus. These little ones, including three more of her own, ease her aching heart. All the girls have two or three children and Sally has another on the way. Fortunately there's a balance between the sexes in this new generation. We know that when they are a little older they will pick their partners from the children in town. There are precious few to choose from but at least they'll have that choice. Their parents didn't. But I see Lou turn white and I feel my own heart clench whenever one of the children sneezes.

Author's note: I wrote this in 2013, long before we'd heard of Covid-19. It's not been edited since.

The Waterfall

Hinckley Hall was said to be haunted. It had changed hands several times in recent years because people couldn't settle there. Some places simply had an aura about them. They had an unnerving effect on those who lived there. Finally it went on the market at a rock bottom price because bad news gets round and nobody wanted to live there anymore.

It was bought by George Graham, a property developer, who was delighted with the place and its spectacular views. Because it was so cheap, he would be able to afford to lavish money on the renovations and he intended to turn the place into a hotel. He planned a spectacular opening with a full-page feature in a glossy lifestyle magazine so that the people with the money would know he was open for business.

His wife, Helena, said he was mad.

"What are you thinking spending all that money on a haunted house?" she asked him. "Nervous people won't come at all and others won't sleep in the haunted room."

"What haunted room?" he asked. "I had a good shufti round when I went to view the place. I'm not daft, you know. I asked the agent which room was haunted. He didn't even know. He'd heard the rumours like everyone else but he didn't know the specifics. Anyway, I managed to contact the seller. The agent wouldn't give me contact details but I know how to use the internet."

"What did he have say, then?"

"He said it was the Blue Room. Lady Sarah Hinckley is supposed to have died in there about three hundred years ago. I went back for another look and I paid special attention to that room. I tell you, I couldn't sense anything."

"I should think you'd have to sleep in the room. Don't ghosts come out at night?"

"I think that's the superstition. Don't believe it myself. I think, once a rumour starts, people are open to suggestion. They think they feel cold or they've heard a creepy noise or something. It's all a load of rubbish."

"I hope you're right!"

The renovation work went on apace and George and Helena decided they needed to be on site to keep the job on track. The rooms were in no state to be lived in so they brought in a caravan. The grounds of Hinckley Hall were magnificent and had been well laid out many years before. Gorgeous lawns swept right up to the front of the hall and were currently being thoroughly trashed by the workmen and their vehicles.

"Oh, look what they've done to the grass!" Helena cried.

"Don't worry," George reassured her. "I've been in touch with a landscape gardener. His outfit will sort it all out for us when the builders have gone. Not a problem, he said."

George liked to be hands-on with his building projects but Helena's skills didn't come into their own until the structural work was finished. She was an interior designer and it would be her job to turn the empty spaces inside into luxurious rooms for those who wanted to be thoroughly spoilt for a few days. She was looking forward to this.

George and his team redesigned the interior of the building, ensuring the plumbing was upgraded and every room had en-suite facilities. They also totally rewired the place so there were enough sockets for modern living. A luxury kitchen ensured that the food they offered would be second to none. While all this was happening and Helena had nothing to do, she took to exploring the grounds.

There was a network of paths that would give their guests some lovely walks without leaving the premises. There was a small lake, a rock garden and even a waterfall. It was all so beautiful. Whenever Helena took the path that led to the top of the waterfall, she felt as though she was coming out of shelter and into the wind. It was up a hill of course, but there was, however still the day, an inexplicable draught. The view from up there was stunning. It was the most elevated point in the grounds and the house stood proud a few hundred yards away. She could see the back of the building from the top of the falls and would go up there to stand in the strange breeze and watch the progress of the build.

"We're gutting the Blue Room today," George told her one morning. "I've still not seen anything ghostly and the lads haven't either. Do you reckon we'll find anything when we rip all that old Anaglypta and thick paint off? What's the betting on a secret room or a bricked-up nun?"

Helena tutted at him and went off for a walk again.

"I'll keep you posted," he yelled after her, laughing.

She let her mind and her feet wander. Perhaps for tradition's sake she would keep that room blue when she redecorated. It would be good to be able to keep the story going for the tourists. In her mind she chose fabrics for the soft furnishings, decided on swags and tails for the curtains and thought she would go for a patterned paper on one wall.

She slowly climbed the rugged path to the head of the waterfall and as she turned from the sheltered side into the usual wind, right at the edge of hearing, she became aware of a sound like a baby's cry. She turned her head this way and that to try and get an idea of direction. She couldn't hear it now. Had it really been there? Such a small sound. Was it in her imagination? Was it just this inexplicable draught?

When she got back, George saw her approaching and went out to her with a spare hard hat in his hand.

"Want to come and look at the haunted room, then?"

"What have you found?" she asked. He wouldn't tell her. He must have wanted her to see for herself.

"But there's nothing here!" she said, twirling around in the middle of the empty, echoing room.

"Exactly!" George said with a smug smile. "Nothing at all. I told you. That 'haunted room' stuff is a load of baloney!"

Certainly, as she looked about her, there was no sign of bricked-up apertures or trapdoors. Nothing to suggest any 'leftover echoes' from the past. Against one of the walls the workmen had propped some lengths of plasterboard to be used in making an en-suite cubicle.

"You've checked under the floorboards?" she asked. George and the two workmen looked at one another.

"Erm... no. I never thought of that."

George tapped the boards with a broom handle, listening in case any sounded different; hollow. One of the lads lifted a couple of boards by the window. They came up easily. There was a slight gust and a puff of dust as the boards came up. Inside was a small piece of cloth. It didn't seem to be anything identifiable. Just some old-fashioned fabric, perhaps cut from a woman's dress long ago. Inside it, carefully wrapped in the dark green, patterned velvet, was a pair of small, black leather shoes. They looked a size or two too small for Helena's feet. A woman's, then, but a petite woman's. Their leather was still soft as a glove and they had slightly elevated heels with a metal edge, presumably to prevent wear.

"Oh, aren't these just sweet?" Helena asked, holding them almost reverently. "We could put them in a display cabinet in

Reception and get the story of the Haunted Room printed up and framed to show next to it. Tourists love that kind of thing!"

"I think you're on to something there," said George. "If it gets to be famous we could even charge more for the Haunted Room. Like a challenge, you know?"

"I think we need to sleep in it first, though. If it's too spooky we can just have it as a sort of ghostly exhibition. Maybe I can find out something about Sarah Hinckley and we can make a feature of it?"

Until the rooms were ready for decoration, Helena continued her walks in the grounds. There was an ideal spot by the lake for a little pavilion. She made some notes to ask George if he thought it was a good idea. It would make a superb photo-spot for weddings. Yes, they could branch out into weddings and functions. She was fired up with ideas. Each time she climbed the path to the top of the falls, she listened for the baby's cry. Her heart beat faster each time she heard it. More often than not when she visited the spot, she heard the little, hiccupping sob of a tiny child.

Eventually, her turn came and though she didn't do the decorating herself, she supervised a team of painters and paper-hangers. Her strengths were in soft furnishings and she chose fabrics, cut and stitched and was able to produce the most opulent effects for a fraction of what they would have paid if they'd bought them in.

They were almost ready to organise their grand opening and, although they had their own rooms in the attic level, Helena insisted they spend a night in the Blue Room, now decorated dramatically in turquoise with accents of chocolate brown. Three of the walls were painted in the blue with a marbled effect and one was hung with a gorgeous paper featuring peacock feathers with gold highlights. The carpet was brown and so thick you could leave footprints in it. Gold fittings in the en-suite added to the feeling of luxury. Helena was pleased with herself.

They settled to sleep. George tried to convince her that if anything supernatural had clung to the small shoes, it would now be transferred to the reception desk and disturb nobody.

The night progressed and George began to snore softly. Helena nudged him awake around 2:00 a.m. to ask if he thought it had gone cold.

"The heating's gone off, love. Of course it's cold."

"Can you hear anything?" she asked, determined to keep him awake and on the alert, as she was.

"Not a dicky bird. Now go to sleep!" he instructed.

Helena heard creaks, groans, the natural settling of a wooden framed house as the temperature changed at night. She started to believe George was right. Then just on the edge of sleep and the borders of hearing, she heard footsteps. She poked poor, long-suffering George again.

"Listen!" Her urgent whisper and the bruise-inducing elbow shattered his sleep again.

"What now?" he muttered. He seemed to be trying to make his brain understand where his body was.

"Footsteps! Can you hear them? Can you hear that gentle 'clop, clop' of footsteps on floorboards?"

"Where the hell's it coming from?" he whispered, his mouth falling open as the sound grew closer, louder.

"It's in this room! But how can it be?" Helena asked. "There's carpet everywhere. You could clomp round here in steel-soled clogs and not be heard."

They lay side by side, rigid and tense, as they heard the footfalls crossing the room, passing right by George's side of the bed and halting at the window. After a few seconds, when they began to release their pent-up breaths, it began again, as though somebody had turned away from observing the view and re-crossed the room, back toward the door.

"*Now* do you think it's haunted?" Helena asked, as the footsteps crossed the room and back a third time, clearly ringing on wooden boards.

"I can't think how else to explain it. I don't believe in ghosts, though."

"You believe your own ears, don't you?" she whispered from the other side of the bed.

Next morning, after a restless night, when each expected another noise, another temperature shift, another heart-thumping fright, they decided to make enquiries about Lady Sarah Hinckley.

"Let's assume she was crossing the room to look out of the window," George said. "What's the view from this window?" He pulled back and tied the drapes carefully – Helena was watching, after all – and stared out across the grounds.

"What's that big hill back there? You walk around the gardens a bit, don't you?"

"It's the hill where the waterfall tumbles into the little lake," Helena said. "That's a bit spooky too."

"You and your 'spooky'! Who ever heard of a haunted waterfall? What does it do? Shriek and drip blood?"

"George, you can be so sarcastic at times. It's not clever and it's not an endearing trait! You didn't believe the room was haunted, did you?"

"I'm still not sure I do but I can't explain it any other way. Alright then, in what way is the waterfall spooky?"

"Will you come with me for a walk and you'll see what I mean? Probably."

"Probably?"

"Well, most times, I hear something. Just occasionally I don't."

They put on their coats and took what was George's first walk around the grounds of his 'almost ready to open' hotel.

"I can't believe you've never wanted to explore this place,"

Helena said. "It's a huge selling point. Think of the wedding-photo opportunities."

They walked hand in hand along the paths, admiring the solitude of the garden and the way its winding tracks gave upon new and unexpected views. Even with dozens, hundreds of people here, you could manage to find a bit all to yourself and imagine you were alone.

They turned a final bend and came upon the steep path which led up the side of the hill to the source of the waterfall.

"Blimey, it's breezy up here all of a sudden!" George said. "I should have put a scarf on."

"It's always like that up here," Helena replied. "Always draughty, chilly. Let's stop and see if we can hear anything." For almost a minute they stood together, the strange little breeze whiffling through their hair.

"Nope! Can't hear any... Is that a baby?" They both turned their heads slightly. From up here it was always hard to tell where the sound was coming from. Helena had tried to trace it so many times without success.

"I think it's coming from down there," said George, pointing down the river of shining water, splashing into a little pool below before running in glistening rills into the lake.

They walked slowly back down the path in silence, straining their ears to hear the sound again. It had quite gone and there was nothing but the chuckling of the water on the stones when they got to the bottom.

"I never hear it anywhere but at the top," Helena said.

"I'm happy to advertise a haunted room," said George. "There are some people that will really fancy that – to tell their mates about. But I think I'll go easy on advertising a haunted waterfall. That's a bit too bizarre!"

The grand opening of Hinckley Hall Country House Hotel was announced in the local press and in the quality glossy magazine with which George had an arrangement. It would take place in a week's time. They had a chef working on menus, a cleaning team ensuring that no builders' dust was left in any dark corners and George had hired gardeners to repair the damaged lawn and tidy up the gardens. They were not exactly neglected but they looked so much better for a bit of pruning and weeding.

Helena had looked on the internet to try to find something about Sarah Hinckley but in vain. Then she thought to look in the local history library. A helpful librarian brought out a couple of ancient books for her and she leafed through, searching for the name.

'Lady Sarah Hinckley. Born 1698; died 1717. Scandal surrounded her death. She was incarcerated in the family Manor House for becoming pregnant out of wedlock. She is said to have killed herself by jumping from her bedroom window. There is no record of the birth or the sex of the child.'

"Yes!" said Helena, then looked around in embarrassment in case anyone had noticed. She was still alone in the room, though. She went through to ask the librarian if she could have a photocopy of the original, which she intended to use for her 'haunting' display, with the small shoes.

She returned to the hotel that afternoon with a look of triumph on her face and a sheet of paper in her hands.

"Look, I think we've got her! It was a tragic suicide. She threw herself from the window of that room!" Suddenly she realised her elation was callous. It was a young girl's life they were talking about. No doubt she was driven by parental cruelty to take such a final step.

"It's going to make a good story for the opening, isn't it?" George said. "Pity we're too late to add it to the glossy. It's gone to press – weeks ago, I think."

"It'll catch the locals and we can include it when we reprint our brochure."

The day before the hotel opened to the public there was a big reception for local business people, the newspapers, the chamber of commerce. Just about everyone George could think of. All was ready apart from last minute titivation in the grounds. One of the lads had decided the stones around the plunge-pool beneath the waterfall were getting mossy and could constitute a slip hazard. He'd taken the big, surrounding stones off, one by one, marked their position on a diagram and scrubbed the moss from them. Then he lifted some of the stones in the bottom of the pool only a couple of feet deep in the centre, so he could take out the pond-weed growing there.

His freezing fingers began to lift out miniature rib bones, a small skull, the whole tiny, pathetic skeleton of a new-born baby.

Gemini

I stood over the inert form of my best friend's partner and watched the trickle of blood seep into a rock pool.

"Layla! What the hell have you done?"

Aimee appeared around the same rock I'd just clambered over and dashed, breathless, to my side.

"What do you mean, 'what have I done'? I've not touched him." My protest sounded whiney and feeble to my own ears as the summer breeze wafted my voice out to sea. My complaint was wasted on Aimee. She dropped to her knees beside Karl, her boyfriend of two years and now her live-in man. Not that I haven't often thought I'd like to deck the self-obsessed, manipulative twerp. But I never would. Not really.

"Quick, grab your phone," she said, feeling his neck for a pulse. I could see it hammering away from where I stood, looking down on them.

"He's fine," I said. "You spoil him. He'll have slipped. Showing off, I suppose."

"You never did like him. You're jealous, just because we used to be so close and now it's him and me. You're so childish, Layla!"

There was a hot silence as she grabbed my phone from my hand to ring for an ambulance. I grabbed it back, sat on a nearby rock and wondered where it had all gone wrong.

***

I've known Aimee since senior school. We were parked next to one another by the teacher on our first day and found we had a lot in common. We saw each other after school and, as we grew older, we often got together at weekends too. We'd catch the bus into town and spend hours at the makeup counters, trying samplers of new lipsticks and perfumes till the assistants told us we had to buy something or leave. We always liked the same things and would turn up to school discos dressed virtually alike. That's how we came to be called The Twins by our other school mates.

We were both born in early June, too, just two days apart. I was first – the elder of the two. We were summer babies, born under the star sign of Gemini, so that was another reason to call us The Twinnies. It was meant as a laugh, of course – a bit like that film with Danny DeVito and Arnold Schwarzenegger. I was the tall, thin, blonde one and Aimee was smaller, not fat, but a little plumper, 'delightfully curvy' as she would say, and her head was a mass of dark, glossy curls. She put these down to her Italian grandparents.

Looks apart, though, we were dead ringers for each other. Our tastes in most things coincided. Most things.

The only difference was our taste in boys. We used to joke that we'd go for the same man and that would break us up. We never did, though. We both had short-lived experimental flirtations with boys, as you do, but nothing serious. I was the first to get a real boyfriend. Jordan was in the year above us at school and I'd always had my eye on him. He was popular with all the girls – except Aimee. He was tall, like me, and athletic, not like me! But Aimee played it cool with him. Frigid, actually. I wondered at first if it was jealousy but no, she seemed genuinely indifferent to him.

Then she met Karl. This was a couple of years later, when

we both had jobs. I never liked him from the off. He was dark, like her, but where she was cheerful and smiling he was always scowling. I never saw him smile – not while I was there anyway. She and I didn't see each other quite so much but our weekends were still spent shopping together in the daytime. Evenings, though, were for our boyfriends.

Sometimes, as we were trying on tops in town, I'd ask what they were doing that evening.

"Dunno yet," she'd reply. "I need to see what Karl fancies."

"Damn him," I'd say, or sometimes I'd put it more strongly. "What do *you* fancy doing? A relationship's a two-way thing, you know."

"Yeah, but I like to go where he wants to go. To please him, you know."

It began to sound altogether manipulative to me. It was as if this Karl wouldn't let her have opinions of her own. She started to choose her clothing differently too. Instead of the bright and blingy stuff we used to love, she'd go for something a bit more staid, 'because Karl likes it'. I called it old-fashioned; she called it classic or subtle or something. I couldn't help but see this as a criticism of my taste, as I was still going for the sparkly stuff and the sequins. When I went out, I liked to dress the part.

"What does Jordan think of your clothes?" she asked one day, as we were pulling stuff off the rails and trying it against ourselves.

"How should I know? He always says I look nice. That's good enough for me. I don't need a complete breakdown of his thought processes, you know. I'm my own woman, Aimee. You should stand up for yourself a bit more. You're getting downtrodden, you know. I don't think it's at all healthy, this obsession you have with pleasing Karl. You're becoming a doormat."

Things went a bit quiet between us for a week or two after

that, but we soon got back to being besties again.

***

It was Easter time when I had my genius brainwave. I rang her up one evening after work and suggested we meet for a coffee. "And don't you dare tell me you have to run it past Karl!" I almost yelled down the phone. She laughed at the idea – yet it was so much the kind of thing she'd been saying recently.

Anyway, we met in the coffee shop and put our heads together over a skinny latte and a slice of cake each.

"I've had this brill idea!" I said. "You know we'll both be twenty-one in June? Well what do you think about a little holiday together, to celebrate? I'm sure we could get a midweek break cheap. Somewhere at the seaside, maybe?"

"Blimey. Great idea. But I'll…"

"… have to ask Karl," I chanted, pulling a face and waggling my head from side to side.

"I was going to say, see if my parents have organised anything for me." She pursed her lips, turned her mouth down and actually made me feel a bit bad. I hadn't even considered that my folks might be doing something special for me.

"Fair point," I agreed. "But that's likely to be at the weekend, isn't it? And anyway, if we get in early, they can work round us. We'll need to book two or three days off work. It'll be great, won't it? Just us, like the old days."

"You mean you don't intend the boys to come, Layla?"

"Not their birthdays, is it?"

"Well, no, but it'd be more fun with them, wouldn't it? What do you say? All four of us. At the coast in June. Best weather of the year, in June."

Actually, now she'd mentioned the lads, I could see it

would be a great laugh, but I didn't want her to think she'd persuaded me. "I'm on my way to tell Jordan about it right now," I said. "I just wanted to run it past you first. You know, to make sure you were up for it."

She lowered her head and looked at me from under her raised eyebrows, just like the teachers at school used to. I don't think I got away with that one. "And Jordan can drive us there. If we want a day out while we're there we can go a bit further afield. It'll be great."

"Won't he mind? I mean, it's a bit like work for him, isn't it?" Jordan's a delivery driver but he always says it's his dream job because he loves driving.

"Of course he won't mind. He can't get enough of engines, you know what he's like. He'll love it. I'll tell him tonight."

So that's what we did. I rang a small hotel at Filey, booked us a midweek break – two double rooms for three nights. I told my mum and dad that we were off to the seaside so that if they wanted to give me a party for my birthday they would have to make it one of the weekends. They looked surprised. Probably because they didn't think I had the nouse to organise something like this for myself.

I got Jordan to take four days of his holidays and of course he said it was fine to take his car. It was ages before Aimee said that Karl was on board with it. Can't think why he wouldn't be if he truly cared for her. Just because it wasn't his idea. He's a right Neanderthal. What do they call it? Alpha Male. Wants to be the one in charge of everything just to show how macho he is, and of course, little Aimee lets him. She's welcome to him.

So that's how we came to be together in Filey for our twenty-first birthdays. It turned out that my mum and dad weren't planning a big party for me – not even when I'd dropped a big hint. We did go out for a posh meal on the Saturday before, though, with my sister, her husband and even my gran, so I wasn't too miffed.

Over the years we'd all been to Filey before but I told Jordan how to get to our small hotel and he delivered us safe and sound. We had two rooms next to one another and the walls were so thin that if we didn't have the telly on I could hear Aimee and Karl talking. I couldn't make it all out but I heard my name a couple of times. They must have been really grateful for me sorting all this out for us.

I'd arranged a meal at a local restaurant the first night. It was good food and we all seemed to enjoy it though I could see that Karl and Aimee were a bit down. Maybe they'd had a row. I hoped she was standing up for herself. After the meal, I grabbed Jordan's hand and told the other two we were off for a moonlit walk – dead romantic, I thought. There are some lovely little walks along the cliffs there and a moonlit walk sounded just the job to get Jordan in the mood.

Day Two was my birthday and I got to choose where we went. Karl – and Aimee, she said – were keen to go on the beach and explore Filey Brig. It's a long rock formation that stretches out to sea. You can walk along it right to the end when the tide's out, but it breaks up into small outcrops as the sea comes in. I told them they could go if they wanted, but for my birthday I wanted to explore the moors. The Brig would still be there tomorrow. And on Friday, Aimee's birthday and our last day.

I could see they felt they were being pressured, but hey, whose birthday was it? We went into the little town to buy the stuff for a picnic lunch. Jordan plonked it into the back of the car and we piled in – in silence. The spoiled brats. Jordan never says much anyway. He likes a quiet life, he says. But Aimee and Karl were distinctly frosty. I don't know why she lets him take advantage of her like this. He can talk her into anything. He's so manipulative. Wouldn't surprise me if he's holding something over her – maybe the threat of breaking up? She'd be better off without him, in my opinion.

Anyway, by the time we found Dalby Forest and its visitor centre, got our picnic unpacked, ate the food and had a lovely walk in the June sunshine, everything seemed alright again. Karl must have come round to my way of thinking.

Thursday, our last full day, was the day it happened. We went down on the beach and messed about in the water for a bit, but it was so bloody cold. The North Sea never warms up. You have to be some special kind of hardy or foolish being to swim in it. We just paddled, splashed each other and then decided to go out on the Brig. After that we were going for fish and chips. There are a couple of decent fish shops there that have little restaurants attached. We were going to be spoilt for choice.

"I'm going over to see what the north side is like," Karl said, striding out.

"Watch your footing," Aimee said. "I'll follow you in a minute. I need to dry my feet and put my shoes back on."

"For goodness' sake," I whispered to her. "You don't have to hold his hand. What's the deal with you two? Why do you have to be with him every minute? I think it's sinister, I really do. I don't know why you aren't more worried about the hold he's got on you."

"It's not like that, Layla. We just enjoy being together. Discussing things, deciding things between us. There isn't one of us in charge, you know."

"Could have fooled me."

She gave me that strange look again. "What?" I asked.

"Nothing. Look, I've got my shoes on now. I'm going up on top to see how far I can get. Maybe right to the end."

I scrambled up first, but Jordan was lolling on the beach, reading a newspaper. "Coming?" I asked.

"Nah. Getting myself psyched up for fish and chips, that's all."

I dashed after Karl. I wanted to see what he was up to. Aimee was happy to pootle around on the rocks this side of the Brig but I wanted to go across and keep an eye on him. He was the unknown quantity to me. And that's when I found him, lying on the rocks with blood seeping into the water nearby.

Aimee saw him from the top of the Brig. She wanted to call for an ambulance. "How the hell do you think it's going to get down here?" I asked. "And look at him. There's nothing wrong with him." Karl was now pushing himself up to his feet, and wincing as he did so.

"Hell. I slipped and caught my hand on one of those rocks." The blood was from his hand, not from a head wound as I'd originally thought. He nursed one hand in the other for a few moments, then wrapped his handkerchief around it. Aimee rushed to tie it for him. "I'm okay, love," he said. "Let's just get our lunch, shall we? We can talk about this afterwards."

I didn't like the sound of that. Talk about it? What was there to say? I hoped she wasn't going to get the blame for this – for wanting to go on the Brig, for example. We trooped in silence off the beach and into the town, looking for one of those fish and chip places we'd seen earlier. As soon as we placed our orders, Aimee and I did the girlie thing of going off to the loo together.

"Aimee," I said, "have you heard of coercive control?"

"Well, yes. But what's that got to do with anything?"

"I think Karl's manipulating you. Does he ever tell you things with no evidence or persuade you that something's happened when it hasn't? You know, gaslighting?"

"I don't know what you're on about, Layla."

"I just think he's got an unnatural control over you. He seems to bend you to his will all the time."

"Bend me to his will? Listen to yourself, will you?"

"You never do anything without his say-so. He's controlling you!"

"Don't be ridiculous, Layla. Where's all this coming from? Are you jealous that he's taken over your role in my life?"

"Taken over… what on earth do you mean?"

"You used to be the one who decided where we went and what we did. You always influenced me as to what to wear. You're still bloody organising everyone right now. You booked it all, you chose the eating places – it's all you, Layla. If anyone's coercive and manipulating, it's you. And you always have been!"

I couldn't have been more upset if she'd actually slapped me in the kisser! I stalked out, dragged Jordan away and made him drive me home. I don't know how Aimee and that stupid Karl of hers got back and I don't care if they never did. I was only trying to help my lifelong best friend and that's the thanks I got! That was the end of a beautiful friendship, you might say. Thank God Jordan still does what I tell him.

Nanna's Knitting

Uncle Joe was the first to die. He hadn't turned up for the family New Year party and everyone was worried. Joe never missed a family do. Eventually, not long before midnight, Dad and I went round to his house to see if he'd fallen asleep or maybe started the celebrations a bit too early and enthusiastically. The frost crunched under our feet as we walked up Joe's front path. Knocking yielded no answer so we used the spare key.

We found Joe just as the midnight bells rang clear over the town rooftops. He was lying on the floor in his hallway, dressed to go out. He'd got all wrapped up for the freezing weather, with a warm overcoat and the scarf that Nanna had knitted. It was wrapped twice around his neck and pulled tight. He'd been strangled. The police could find no evidence of a break-in. He couldn't have strangled himself, could he? Eventually he'd black out, slacken his grip and breathe again. Surely?

Three days later Aunty Lizzie found my cousin Dan spark out on the bedroom floor. She pushed him with her foot to rouse him. Teenagers can sleep anywhere. He wouldn't wake, though. She screamed the place down when she realised he was dead. He had bruises around his throat which corresponded to finger-marks. His own finger-marks. He was wearing his Christmas fingerless gloves from Nanna.

Nanna was nearly blind but she could knit up a storm. She did it by touch and so long as Aunty Jane stitched things up for her, she continued to use the simple patterns she'd memorised as a child. She would cast on by feel and count the rows by running her sensitive finger ends over the ridges of the plain knitting she always did. She'd made everyone gifts that year, all with the same indigo wool.

My mother was the last to go. I heard her collapse upstairs and ran to see what the noise was. Her face was flushed dark red, her eyes and ears were leaking blood and she struggled weakly like a landed fish for just a few seconds before the bobble hat from Nanna crushed her skull.

It was ridiculous. The police and the coroner could establish no connection other than the presence of an item of Nanna's Christmas knitting. I had a scarf which I'd unwrapped but not yet worn. I knew I wouldn't wear it now. We burned all the other presents and I was in her house when the police went to see her. She had another scarf part done when they entered so she stopped and put it away to talk to them. She wound the wool round and round then pushed her two needles up into the ball so they just poked out of the top. Popping the knitting in her work bag, she flashed the officers a cheery smile, oblivious to the carnage arising from her sedate pastime. One officer paused mid-question. The bag had just moved.

A Moment in Time

It happened when I decided to take a shortcut. I knew the general direction so I turned off the busy road and drove along a narrow country lane between tall hedges creamy with elderflowers. It was high summer and, unusually for this part of the country, it was a delightful summer's day. It was sunny, warm and there was a light breeze making the air temperature tolerable.

As I drove slowly, taking the many sharp curves carefully, I saw an old-fashioned horse-drawn cart coming towards me. The horse had its mane plaited with ribbons, and wild flowers were intertwined with the coarse hair. The couple sitting behind it were dressed in antique style clothing, he in a stiffly formal brown suit, she in an off-white, long-skirted dress adorned with heavy, cream lace the colour of the elderflower heads in the hedgerow.

The farm cart, for such it seemed to be, left the roadway, which at this point had become rather unkempt and more like a green lane. It turned into a field entrance and, puzzled, I continued to the next suitable parking place and halted. I wondered what was going on. I got out of the car and made my way back towards the turning they'd taken. I was intrigued by their weird attire and wanted to know what was happening. Was it some kind of pageant? Why were they dressed so strangely?

I walked into what I thought was a field and found a small, stone-built chapel surrounded by closely cut grass. A group of people, all dressed in that same old-fashioned style, spilled out onto the steps before the church door, smiling in the mid-morning sunshine. I was puzzled. They looked like film extras for some movie about the Amish or the Mennonites. There were no cars, just a few tethered horses and the cart that I'd followed.

I watched as the group gathered on the steps as though for a photograph but no equipment was in evidence. There was nobody organising the bride and groom and their guests. It was as though they struck an instinctive pose as they emerged, blinking in the bright air.

My instinct was to hang back in the shade of the shrubs that formed the field hedge. I saw the original couple taking wooden boxes and wicker baskets from the cart and ferrying them round to the right hand side of the chapel where two men were setting up boards on trestles to form a long table. They were having the wedding party right here in the field.

The older women spread cloths on the boards and laid out the food which consisted of a quantity of bread rolls, big bowls of fruit, a great wheel of cheese and a huge ham which the parson or vicar had set to carving into chunky slices. All the girls had flowers in their long hair and the children were running around the table, laughing. It reminded me of a televised film of a Thomas Hardy story.

One little girl broke away from her friends, dashed to the table and snatched up a piece of fruit. She ran right past me and held her hand out flat to one of the horses tethered there, grazing. It raised its head and blew a huffling greeting to her, then lowered its head to accept the large strawberry on her palm, taking it with its soft lips. She leaned towards it and rubbed the length of its nose.

As she turned, her gaze slipped past mine. "Hello," I said. "Whose wedding is this?" She continued turning, ignoring my presence completely. Frustrated, I reached for the horse to pet it as she had. My hand and the horse's long nose occupied the same space. I couldn't say my hand passed through it, but I couldn't feel it; couldn't stroke it or connect with it. I could see it; I could feel the heat from its body but I couldn't touch it.

I turned from the horse, so substantial and strong, yet untouchable, and approached the group, now seated around the long table, laughing, chatting and passing food along to one another. Was nobody aware of me? I tried to speak to an old man at the end of the table but couldn't attract his attention. I should have felt afraid but instead was merely frustrated. There had to be a rational explanation.

I gave up trying to interact with the strange, antique group and made my way back to the car. Pulling out of the field gateway, I continued down the road in my original direction. The surface became more pitted and grassy as I progressed and I pulled to a halt where the green lane met another flower-strewn hedge. It was a dead end. There was no way out, yet I could hear the traffic on the B road across the field. Now I would have to turn around. Some short cut this was turning out to be.

Back down the lane, I once again passed the opening to the chapel. It was sealed by a modern farm gate with a length of chain and a padlock. Risking blocking the road, though in truth I'd seen no traffic here other than the now vanished cart, I pulled up and went to look. The field was populated by sheep and the chapel itself nothing but tumbled stones. Now I was scared.

I climbed the gate and walked over to the shattered steps where, moments before, I'd watched a wedding party assemble, then turned to the grassy sward where they'd set out the simple feast. How could that be? I almost felt that, by straining my hearing, I could have caught the merry laughter of the children.

I returned to my car and made my way back towards the road from which I'd originally turned off. Once again, the road surface beneath my wheels gradually deteriorated and I found myself parked against a hawthorn hedge. I couldn't get out.

I made my mind up to go back and, if necessary, barge my way through the hedge on foot to get to the civilised sounds of traffic I'd heard in the distance. Shaking, I crunched the gears as I clumsily turned the car, almost rolling into one of the ditches. Passing the chapel field again, I kept my eyes on the rough road surface, not daring to challenge my senses with the sight, whatever it should turn out to be.

Gradually the road surface improved until I was once again driving on grey tarmac, albeit with a seam of grassy growth down the centre of its single track. Only when I rounded the last bend and saw the T junction ahead did I realise I'd been holding my breath. I was out, free. I was no longer trapped.

Shaking, I pulled out into the stream of traffic and as soon as I could, I found a lay-by where I parked and turned off the engine. In spite of the sunny day, the bright hedgerows, decked with elder, honeysuckle and pink dog-rose flowers, I was shivering. I knew I wasn't fit to drive. I got out of the car and, taking a few deep breaths, I walked up and down for a few minutes until I felt capable of driving home, the original purpose of my journey forgotten in the buzz of terror.

Two days later I heard the news that my grandmother had passed away. She had been ancient forever to my eyes and I now learnt that she'd been close to 100 years old on her death. My mother passed all the family paperwork to me, with a request to scan anything of significance and save them to a disk so family around the country could have a copy.

My parents' wedding photograph was there with its dated fashions. Grandmother's picture was there too, all black and white and formal. Her own parents had even had a photograph taken, a rare thing in those days. Great-granny, the bride, stood with my great-granddad, in a stiff and formal arrangement of figures. The exposure time required back then would have been several seconds, so they seemed to be frozen in time.

Great-granny's own parents and grandparents stood formally behind her and in the eyes of her grandmother I saw with a shock the creased and aged face of the little girl who, a few days previously, had fed strawberries to a long-dead horse.

Dead End

It has been reported in some of the more dubious press outlets that 3.7 million Americans believe they have been subjected to alien abduction. Ridiculous. Why would aliens choose one nationality above others? I know that they don't. They took me.

I lost a week from my life earlier this year. I went to bed as usual and when I woke I assumed it was the following morning. I felt a bit sore but otherwise I had no reason to think anything was amiss. People asked where I'd been when I went into work 'next day' and I didn't know what they were talking about. Reality came back slowly, like the snatched morning memories of nightmare.

I went to bed one night and woke, sedated and partially anaesthetised, in a gleaming laboratory staffed with metal 'workers'. I never knew where it was situated: on Earth, on a ship: on another planet? An ovum was removed from my body and returned fertilised. I was left alone then, but for the metal beings which brought me food and drink and removed my waste products with mechanical efficiency. My belly swelled at a frightening rate and three days later the true nightmare began.

The hot, tight mound of my abdomen began to lurch and writhe. It appeared that the gestation period was mercifully short. I lay upon the couch, groaning as my body tried to wrench itself apart. I was mortally afraid. I did not see any of my abductors so, thank god, I didn't know what the father of the hybrid child looked like. I struggled to expel it, screaming both in pain and in rage at the violation of my body.

With one final lurching contraction I expelled the monster in a slurry of stinking mucous and it lay, writhing and tormented, between my trembling thighs. It was unnaturally thin and long and had been curled, folded, within me. It stretched and opened a ghastly mouth ringed with needle-like teeth and I could immediately see that there was no throat, no oesophagus. This thing could not feed! I felt elated and hoped they would discard this as a failed hybridisation experiment.

They returned me to my bed at home but the horror is not yet over. Unwilling to admit defeat, the alien beings seem bent upon keeping this creature alive, perhaps to backcross it and introduce some element of its genetic make-up into their moribund species. I am not expected to feed it as I would a human child. Thank god! But they return it to me every night to clutch at my body, lie along the length of me in a travesty of a human hug, and leach the life-force from my body as it grasps me with its cold, sticky limbs.

This cannot go on. I am losing weight and will not live much longer. When I die, it will die too, this hybrid disaster; this evolutionary dead end. I am happy, on both counts.

Dark Fires

How did it come to this? How did Amy Hall come to wake this morning, stiff and uncomfortable, on a hard bed in a police cell? She was brought here last night and was going to be questioned about a serious crime, they said. About setting fires, damaging property and endangering life. Her mum and dad would have been so angry with her. So ashamed. At least they'd been spared that.

Her twin brother Simon wouldn't be surprised, of course. He had always treated her as though she were thick. He'd tell her off, like a parent would a recalcitrant child. But she wasn't. She was just not as quick as he was. She could think things through and get the right answer if he gave her the chance. But he wouldn't. Now she was in so much trouble with the law they may never let her out of here. Maybe he was right. She was just stupid.

She sat down on the hard bench again and put her head in her hands. She wasn't cold but she was shaking. Shaking so thoroughly that her teeth ached in her jaw as she clenched it. What was going to happen to her? Her life had gone totally wrong.

***

A police officer came in with a breakfast of sorts, and told Amy she'd be getting a visit from the duty solicitor. She'd read enough and seen enough TV to suggest to her that this meant she really was a suspect and would be questioned, perhaps arrested. She asked the officer if her brother had been in contact, looking for her. Had Simon missed her yet? Had he even bothered to ring around to try to find her? If he found she was in here – had been here all night… The officer was indifferent to her pleas. Nobody had rung, he said.

Amy wanted a shower. She wanted a change of clothes and her toothbrush. Whoever this solicitor was, she wanted to meet him feeling at least human, if not good.

The officer brought her out of the cell and into a small, unpleasant room, where another young woman sat at a nasty, cheap-looking table. The air in the room wasn't fresh. It smelt as though lots of sweaty bodies had been in there and it hadn't been aired in between. The woman wore a sober black trouser suit but the buttery yellow blouse underneath it lit her face. Amy felt a little less intimidated. The woman stood and shook her hand. "Hi, I'm Lucy, the duty solicitor this morning. I'll be here when the police question you."

Amy gave a small smile, uncertain of how to treat this woman. Lucy asked the officer for a few moments to speak to her client alone. He locked them in, Amy noticed.

"First of all, can you tell me a bit about yourself?"

***

A little hesitantly, Amy began to let Lucy in on the secrets of her very sheltered life.

"My brother will kill me. He looks down on me in every way," she began.

Lucy listened carefully, taking notes as Amy told her about her life to date. Simon would know there was something wrong by now. She was twenty-eight years old and she'd never stayed away from home before, not for a single night. He'd be wondering what had happened to her. He'd be worried to death, until he found out. Then she'd come in for the sharp edge of his anger. He'd hate her to bring the spotlight onto them. The two of them, single people living alone since their parents' early death in a road accident. He hated her to draw attention to herself. To either of them.

It had started in the womb, though Amy didn't go into this amount of detail to the solicitor. She had visions of Simon elbowing her in her tiny ribs to get to the cervix before she did. As soon as the contractions began, he would want to be first. He'd demand it. Even as an infant, Simon was, to be blunt, a bully.

They were born early and small, as many twins are. Naturally, he was the bigger of the two. Four pounds and six ounces, to her three pounds and two ounces. Her mother told them about it when they were young. Twins, but not completely alike because, of course, one was a boy and one a girl. She discovered later that, as fraternal twins, they were no more alike than any other two siblings. Mum had told her that she'd catch up as she got older but she never did. Simon was a big boy who became a big man. She, though resembling him facially, was an undersized baby who became a dainty, petite woman.

She stood no chance against him. That three minutes difference that made him the older child gave him a huge sense of entitlement. The extra weight and inches in height as a toddler allowed him to push to the front and shove her out of the way whenever he saw anything he wanted. Their parents gave in to him too. He was the firstborn, the clever child, the wonder boy. She was – the also ran. She was loved.

She was definitely not neglected. Yet everything there was to be gained, bought, enjoyed and glorified was Simon's. And 'dear little Amy, such a sweet little thing' was deemed to be lacking compared to him.

As an adult he took to going to the gym, which made the difference even more marked. She'd suppressed a small smile when someone even bigger had broken a tooth for him, but he'd even made that look good by having a gold one fitted. Flash bugger.

As they'd grown older and their parents had passed, Simon insisted to her that she was 'simple', 'backward', needed help to live. They'd left school as soon as they could and, as she'd been in the same class as her brother, she'd always been in his shadow. Only their English teacher, Miss Birch, had seen a spark in Amy. She loved writing essays, especially fiction. Her grasp of language and her vocabulary were excellent, Miss Birch said. Truly, that was the only subject in which she exerted herself. She was better at it than Simon, but she soon discovered it was best not to point that out to him. The only success in her life and she made light of it. With every other school subject, he crowed about his successes and rubbed her nose in her failure. She could have done better in her exams, she knew that, but she'd have suffered for it if she had. She'd learned to repress her own life in the service of her brother's.

They were eighteen when their parents died, together, in the same car accident. Just like that, her home life changed. Simon was now definitely her keeper.

He'd got a decent job after school. He'd worked his way up since, and was now on good pay in a bank. She, with his pushing, and her parents' total indifference, had taken a 'little job' as Simon termed it, in a small local convenience store. Long hours, rubbish pay, but, as he reminded her, that was all she was worth. With constant repetition, she'd come to believe it. She tried to let Lucy know that her brother was the leader, she the mindless follower. The scribbled notes flew over the page.

***

"I'll ask the police to contact your brother later, if he hasn't found out where you are," Lucy said. "That bit of background is interesting, Amy. But now I need to ask a few questions about what you were doing right before the police apprehended you. They have their reasons for bringing you in and questioning you. I need to know if there's anything you should tell them, or perhaps, anything you should keep quiet about."

"What? Lie to the police? Won't that get me into more trouble?"

"You don't need to lie, Amy. Let's just say you don't actually have to tell them everything. Not if it will make things look worse than they really are."

"How can they look worse? I've never been in a police station before and now I've spent the night here – and they still won't let me go home."

"Try to stay calm. It won't help if you make yourself flustered. Just tell me about last night and we'll get our story straight."

Amy told her about the walk. Most evenings Simon insisted they have a little walk together. She was standing all day in her job so she often didn't feel like walking, but his job was sedentary so he felt it did them good to stretch their legs. He told her the blood would pool in her feet if she didn't get them moving. For a quiet life, she went along with it.

Last night they'd just gone around by the local shopping mall. Simon was a smoker but never in the house. Their mother's insistence on the dangers of passive smoking, and the selfishness of smoking where others were – where they had no option but to be – must still have echoed in his head. He would smoke in the garden before work. She had no idea what he did at work – probably they had some outdoor shelter or something – but the evening walk was the chance to light up and he usually got through two, maybe even three, in the course of an evening.

"There was a fire at the mall last night, wasn't there?" she asked Lucy.

"Didn't you know?"

"I could smell smoke, but I often could. And I heard sirens, but that's not unusual. The fire station's close by. Simon's cigarettes, sometimes people's barbecues. The sharp smell of his lighter as he lit up. I'm probably more sensitive to it than people who smoke. I don't think it was always tobacco he was smoking either. It had a funny smell sometimes. Leafy. I can't describe it."

"What happened then?"

"Well, he usually disappeared for a smoke. He didn't want me to breathe any in, even outdoors, he said. He was really considerate like that."

"And you didn't light any fire?"

"What with? I don't have a lighter or matches. I told you, I don't even like other people smoking."

***

The officer came back in at that point, accompanied by a female colleague and they introduced themselves to Amy and Lucy. DS Barker, the lady, and DC Cornish, the man.

"We're going to interview you now, Miss Hall, and we'll be cautioning you and recording the interview, just so there are no mistakes made later."

After DC Cornish had spoken into the machine and given

the details, date and time, he began to ask Amy questions.

"Can you tell us where you were last night, Miss Hall?"

Amy cast a nervous glance at Lucy who nodded to her to carry on.

"I was having a walk near Brook Street Shopping Mall. But I didn't do anything!"

"Do you know why you were brought here?"

"You think I lit a fire there, don't you?"

"And did you, Miss Hall?"

"Of course I didn't! I don't even have anything to light one with. You searched me when you brought me in, didn't you? You took my phone, my watch and my little bit of pocket money."

"Pocket money?"

"Yes, the bit of cash my brother lets me have."

"Do you work, Miss Hall?" asked DS Barker. Her voice was gentle and low, and Amy felt comforted by it.

Amy told them where she worked and how long she'd been there. She also explained that she had to give her brother all her wages each week to look after for her. He gave her a few pounds back, for herself. She didn't miss the look the police officers exchanged.

"What? Is there something wrong with that?"

DC Cornish took over again. "It's not usual, shall we say. But it's not against the law if you consent. Now can you tell us why you were hanging around for so long in that area? You were caught on CCTV in that vicinity, just standing on the corner for several minutes. You walked into shot, then hung around for a while, and then you walked off again. Shortly afterwards, someone called the fire service and us. A suspicious fire, just near where you were waiting."

"I was waiting for Simon. My twin brother."

"Why didn't he appear on the camera, then?"

"He likes to have a smoke in the evening when we go for a

walk. He's very kind to me, you know. He doesn't like to think I'll be breathing in his old smoke. He takes himself off for a bit while he has his cigarette, so I just wander around or stand and wait for him. Usually he'll say, 'Stand over there, Amy, then I can find you. Don't wander off and get lost.' He looks after me, you see."

The two officers stood and spoke into the machine. They were halting the interview for a while, and offered Amy and her solicitor a hot drink. Amy accepted, but Lucy said she'd drunk their brew before and preferred to wait.

"What have I said wrong?"

"It doesn't mean you've said anything wrong, Amy. They must feel they need to check something. Maybe the camera footage again, or perhaps they want to talk to a witness. Don't always assume you're in the wrong."

"I usually am, according to my brother."

It seemed to be a long time later that the two officers returned, DC Cornish spoke into the recorder again, and they resumed their questions.

"Miss Hall," said the sergeant. Lucy had told her that the lady was the senior of the two.

"Yes? You can call me Amy, if you like."

"Thank you, Amy. We have checked CCTV footage from a couple of similar, unsolved fires in the area over the last few months."

Amy wrinkled her brow. "Yes?"

"You appear on all of them." Amy looked blankly at them, then at the solicitor.

"What does that mean?"

"You don't have to say anything," said Lucy, touching her lightly on the arm.

"But they need to find out what happened!" Amy was keen to help and a little dubious about any advice not to do so.

Over the next half hour or so, they managed to establish

that, although Amy was hazy on the dates, she knew she'd been to both these places recently. "We walk almost every night, you know. Simon says it's good for us."

They showed her a couple of clips from the camera footage. "Do you recognise yourself on these?" asked DC Cornish.

"Yes, yes that's me." Lucy looked down at her notes, Amy noticed. Not that she was checking anything. She just didn't seem to want to meet Amy's eye.

"Oh look! And there's Simon!" In one of the other two clips a man could be seen walking away from her as she stood on a street corner, near an arcade.

The officers leaned in closer. "Are you certain?" asked DS Barker. "It's a distant shot. It wouldn't stand up as evidence in court."

"But I know my own brother, Sergeant. I know the way he walks, the coat he always wears, that heavy little leather bag he always takes out with him. Believe me, it's Simon. I remember that night. He said he was going for a smoke and we'd just passed a nice bench. I said I'd sit on that and wait for him, but he kept looking around, like he always does. He said it was no good there. He needed me to wait by the corner."

"Where the camera is…" muttered Cornish. "I think we need to go and have a word with your brother. We'll get someone to bring you a sandwich while you wait."

Lucy had to go, she said, but advised Amy not to admit to anything while she was gone. She'd try to come back later and see if she could help. "What can I admit to if I've not done anything?" asked Amy. "Everything will be alright, you'll see. Simon will make sure I'm okay."

Amy was left alone with her sandwich in the locked room for a while. Someone fetched her another cup of the nasty tea, but it was better than nothing.

Some time later, perhaps a couple of hours, she thought, though she had to guess as she didn't have her watch, the officers returned and resumed the interview. Lucy came back in with them, looking as if she'd been rushing.

"There was nobody at your house," said the constable. "The back kitchen window was open a little so we entered to search for your brother. He is a person of interest in our enquiry. We found no sign of him, no sign that either of the beds had been slept in. We did find some other things, however."

"His smoking stuff?"

"Can you explain what you mean by that, Miss Hall?"

"Well, I know he has a lot of disposable lighters. He makes me buy them from work. On a card. A lot at a time." She gave a small smile. "I can't think how he uses so many when he only has a couple of cigarettes each evening, and one before work. You probably found his other stuff too. His weeds, I think he calls them."

"Are you aware that there is a considerable quantity of petrol in your shed?" asked DS Barker, her voice once again confiding and low.

"Well, yes. Simon uses it for the mower. We share the jobs, you see. He does the shopping – apart from the lighters – because he likes to decide what we're eating. He gets me to cook it. That and the cleaning are my jobs. He does the garden. Well, cuts the grass. There's not much else there." She gave a little laugh. "As you'll have seen."

"He seems to tell you what to do rather a lot, doesn't he?" cut in DC Cornish.

"I suppose he's a bit bossy but since our parents died in that car accident when we were eighteen, he's taken over and looks after me. He thinks I can't look after myself."

"Can you?"

"I think I could. I wouldn't do things the same as he does,

but, you know – a quiet life and all that. He isn't stupid, like me. He's the one who drives and has the good job. He had just passed his test in the family car before the accident. That time when the brakes failed and our parents died. I'd not been allowed to take lessons by then. And now I doubt I shall. Simon won't let me. He says I can't be trusted."

"Did anyone establish why the brakes failed on your family car, Amy?" asked DS Barker.

"I don't know. Simon might know. I'm useless with mechanical stuff. He knows about all that kind of thing. Even before he started driving lessons he used to do the car maintenance. You could, on those old models, he said. None of this computer stuff on our old car. So he'd know, probably."

Amy's clear stare held theirs as she looked enquiringly from one officer to the other. "I wonder why he wasn't home? Do you think he was out looking for me? He'll be really worried. He never lets me go anywhere without him. And you could be sure he hadn't been in his bed because if he had it'd be rumpled. I make them nice and tight each morning. He says I'm very good at it." Once again she smiled at them.

Then her brow clouded. "He must have been out all night looking for me, do you think? He'll be so worried. And if he wasn't, then I'm really worried about him. He's, what do you call it, a missing person? Can I report him missing? Will you let me give you a description?"

"That would be useful, Amy," said the sergeant. "We're really anxious to speak to him at the moment. I think we can let you go back home now, but give DC Cornish a description before you go. Any distinguishing features he has. We'll give you back your belongings and if Simon returns, we'd like you to ring us right away. Can you do that?"

"Yes, of course. I wish he'd come home or ring here. Then he'd know I was alright, wouldn't he?"

"Yes, of course. We'll send DC Gowans, a family Liaison Officer, with you initially. There's the possibility that you're in danger. It will be a bit of company while you're waiting."

After describing her brother, Amy signed for her belongings, fastened on her watch and popped the few items in her pockets. As she left, she heard DC Cornish mutter, "Poor lass." Then a word that sounded like "Gaslighting."

DC Gowans drove her home and disappeared into the kitchen to make tea. Amy had to ring Myra at work to tell her she'd be in tomorrow but that something had happened to stop her coming in today. Myra didn't push it. She rarely bothered to get an explanation from Amy, seeming to regard her as almost sub-normal, but a trustworthy hard worker all the same.

Amy began methodically tidying the house, checking the contents of the fridge and cupboards, making a list for shopping. DC Gowans kept out of her way but Amy felt a little better for knowing she was there. It was some time later in the day that a sharp knock sounded on the door and she opened it to DS Barker and DC Cornish on her front step.

"Hello? Am I in trouble? Do you need me at the station again?" She gave a flustered look from one to the other.

"May we come in?" asked the sergeant. "We'd like to talk to you for a few moments."

She showed them into the neat living room and indicated the sofa and chairs. "Would you like to sit down?"

"Thank you. I think you should sit too," said Barker, as Amy seemed to loiter in the doorway, DC Gowans at her shoulder.

She sat in one of the big, comfortable easy chairs. She was so tiny it almost swallowed her up.

"We're sorry to tell you that we've found some human remains in the basement of that shopping mall. It seems that the fire was started in the lift, as it stood stationary in the basement, with something jamming the door open so it couldn't be called from another floor. From the description of your missing brother, we fear it could be him."

Amy gasped and began to shake. If possible she seemed to become even smaller. "Simon? Can you be sure?" The sergeant had taken the lead here, and she hadn't heard a word from Cornish.

"He has the gold tooth you described, and fits Mr Hall's size. May we take some of his personal belongings to try for a DNA sample?"

"Well, yes." Amy took a long, shuddering breath. "Take whatever you want." Her eyes began to well up and she hunched her shoulders and sniffed hard, wiping her eyes with a sleeve.

"We can leave DC Gowans here with you, so you're not on your own. Or would you like us to ring a family member to stay with you for a while?"

"Oh. I'm not sure. It's always only been me and Simon, since the accident. I don't think I'd like anyone else here now. I'd like to be alone. It's a lot to take in."

"We'll come back if we have any further news, and of course, you'll ring us if we're mistaken and Mr Hall turns up at home, won't you?"

"Yes. Yes, of course. Thank you." Amy took some more deep breaths. She stood, still shaky, and showed the officers to Simon's room. They'd been in both the bedrooms, of course, when they searched the house.

Cornish bagged a comb and a toothbrush, and a woollen hat which seemed to have a few hairs inside. "We'll get these tested," he said, his first words since he'd come into the house. "Any news and we'll be in touch."

Amy muttered another quiet word of thanks, nodding in particular to DC Gowans. She wiped her eyes with the back of her hand as she showed the officers to the door.

"Please, don't hesitate to call us if you think we can help in any way," said DS Barker.

Shivering, Amy watched them go down the path, get into their cars and drive away. She fought the impulse to wave. Closing the door, she leaned back and shut her eyes with a long, shuddering sigh. Deep breathing restored her slightly. She put her hands over her face and made a small whimpering sound.

Relief.

Freedom!

The first fire had given her such a rush of power. She'd noticed how empty these places were just before they closed. It had been worth all the planning, hiding a plastic bag containing petrol, lighters, rags soaked in petrol. She heard the sirens, later in the evening, read about the fire in the local paper and couldn't wait to do it again, a few weeks later. Simon had depleted her life of power. He had taken away everything.

This time, on this last occasion, he must have followed her. She was sure he was sloping off when he left her, not only to smoke but to talk on the phone to that married woman he was involved with. He assumed she was too stupid to know. She always had at least fifteen minutes to get back in place. But this time, he followed her. He caught her leaving the lift, the fledgling flames licking up behind her, and a look of horrified surprise on her face. What he didn't catch was the lump of rock in her hand. She swiped him on the head with it, dragged his limp body into the lift and chocked the door open with her rock.

That would be the last of the fires, of course. Even those dark fires smouldering in her heart. She was glad. Satisfied. She'd never believed her parents' death was an accident, but who would believe little, stupid Amy? He had undermined her at every turn. Never again, though.

Fires all accounted for.
Arsonist killed in the last one.
Case closed.

Deus ex Machina

Ellen had been a nurse in this hospital for sixty years, since long before the shortage of doctors and nurses. Can you believe there used to be several nurses on a ward? Real nurses - flesh and blood like her. And there was a doctor's round every day. I bet you don't even know what that means. A real doctor would come round to each ward, accompanied by the senior nurse, to see how each patient was doing.

And get this! There were different doctors for different ailments. Doctors for bones, doctors for skin complaints, doctors for hearts and livers and kidneys. The human mind can't contain enough information for there to be just one kind of doctor in a hospital. They even had doctors for different kinds of cancer. You may not have heard of that but it was a killer, and much feared back then.

What a leap forward we made when we began to program machines as diagnostic tools. You just put in the information and out came the results. It would tell you what was wrong with you and then give you a recommended treatment. Eventually we improved them sufficiently that they actually administered the treatment, too.

Even before those medi-robots became common, there was already a decline in hospital staff numbers. Who'd work those hours for so little pay? When my friend Ellen started work, medical personnel were looked up to. They were treated as professionals and they had some status in society. Look at us now. Working for the machines.

"Whatever's happened?" I asked. When I called around to meet Ellen as usual after work she wasn't there. I asked the reception terminal, which told me in its silky, reassuring tones that she'd had a little mishap. I'd not been there half as long as Ellen had but I knew a euphemism when I heard it. Oh, we'd taught our robots so well. Even these minor machines, so low in the pecking order, could take on the aspect of the concerned professional. It - though it sounded like a she and we tended to give them female names - tried to sound as though there wasn't a problem.

A slight mishap was nicking your finger and drawing blood. It was tripping and grazing your knee. How did these machines manage to sound so plausible? Because we taught them all we know about dissembling, covering up, outright lying, that's how. Oh, we taught them so well. I went up to the ward, leaving in my wake the chatter of the reception terminal which was sounding, if it's possible for a machine to do so, fretful and anxious. If it could have stopped me it would have done so. I entered the ward and looked for my friend.

It was a standard medical ward, with open-ended cubicles and a central track down which the AI doctor could travel. We'd experimented with bipedal Artificial Intelligences, mainly, I suspect, to make us feel more comfortable with them. In a hospital, though, the AI on its rails whizzing up and down between beds was the most efficient. Bipedal robots were unstable. In the physical sense, I mean.

As on the unit where I worked, there was only one human nurse to every half dozen wards since the AI doctors did everything but the dirty work. The patients were plugged and wired to consoles at the end of their cubicles. The machine whirled silently between beds, checking, monitoring, keeping a watch over the patients and administering the necessary medications.

From entering the hospital to being discharged, the patient was dealt with almost entirely by machines. We 'nurses' were there to remove human waste, dispensed as it was into hygienic containers, and to ensure the medic AIs were topped up with the required drugs. We didn't even have to bring tea round, though we tried to give the sympathy. All nutrients were administered to the patients by the same robot doctor that gave the drugs, worked out the doses and switched on the exercise and massage capability of the high-tech hospital beds.

I looked around for Ellen, expecting to see her in a chair, nursing a bruise. She was nowhere to be seen. I checked her other wards but couldn't locate her. Eventually I did what the visitors did. I typed her name into the wards' central computer unit. She was in bed 15 of Ward 3. Orthopaedic.

Her parents would have been surprised that she was still working here at over eighty years of age. Oh yes, the retirement age continues to rise. People live longer and remain healthier. If we hadn't controlled the birth rate as ruthlessly as we have we'd be in a serious state of overcrowding by now. But these days, eighty-three is no age at all.

There she was. I'd followed the AI's trackway to Ward 3 and found my robust friend Ellen lying, pale, her eyes closed, looking like bruises in her face, with the medi-bed read-outs flashing on the console at the end of her cubicle.

"What on earth's happened here?" I asked. Naturally, no human member of the nursing staff answered me. She had been the only human carer in the group of six wards.

"Mrs Benfold tripped when removing a patient's blanket," said the soft, soothing voice of the AI doctor that I hadn't even heard coming up behind me.

"How is she?"

"She has suffered a fracture of the femur head. She is currently in no discomfort."

That hadn't really been what I'd meant. "Will she be alright?" I asked, no doubt with a little pleading in my voice. I'd heard patients' relatives do that. Beg for reassurance.

"She will be fine," the comforting voice told me. "All shall be well."

I wandered around the ward, checking on Ellen's other patients, greeting them and chatting. It was almost time to allow their visitors to enter.

The AI retreated as the ward was overrun with relatives coming to see their family and friends. So familiar, this. It happened twice a day on my own wards. Visitors came and entered the small cubicles. I heard the voices chattering as the patients sat up to greet friends and family. I went in to sit with Ellen but she was still unconscious, her breathing so shallow I had to keep checking she was still with me.

How long had I been working at this hospital and yet I had never seen anyone die? Surely in thirty years I should have seen a patient die. I did not believe that the machines were so clever, these Artificial Intelligence doctors, that they could stave off death completely. Did these people all die on the night shift? I never knew who came and took over after my working day ended.

Ellen's eyes flickered for a moment then her gaze extended to the small, impersonal cubicle, the wires, the machines. She looked stunned.

"What happened, Ellen?" I asked in a low voice. There was no point assuming the machine wouldn't hear. Of course it would. It monitored all the patients but was aware of visitors in a way that suggested an auditory capacity far beyond that of any human.

"Jenny? Is that you?" Her voice was a whisper, a feeble croak.

"Yes," I said, and took her hand gently. "Are you in any pain?"

"No, no pain," came the whispered response, but the dosage which was automatically fed into her veins to ensure this outcome also dulled her thinking.

"What happened?" I repeated.

"I… I fell. I tripped, I think, over a blanket."

"Reception said you'd broken your hip. I assume they'll operate?"

Her eyes closed in the effort to call up a reply. Then the cubicle whispered in the soothing voice of the AI doctor. "We are monitoring Mrs Benfold's condition and will take suitable action. She is still in shock. We will give her time." I worked with the damned things and still had to stop myself from saying 'thank you' to them.

As the visiting time drew to a close, the cubicle lights dimmed. I could see Ellen needed sleep and all her other requirements were being met by the machine. As I left, I wondered who had been sent to replace her. There didn't seem to be another human on the six wards. No doubt there'd be a replacement sent for the day shift, which was her usual work rota.

Back home, I worried. I always worried – it was my defining quality. Ellen was going to need some months off work. A broken hip, at any age, requires healing time. She was strong, though. She'd cope. She'd helped me when I first started and if I could help her now, I would. As I fell asleep I continued to puzzle over the lack of deaths at the hospital. I'd been there all my working life. Why had I never noticed?

I went in to work early the next morning so I could look in on Ellen before I started my shift. She still lay pale and inert, sleeping her way to health, I hoped. I looked for the AI doctor but the machine was tending another patient, this one a gentleman with an arm injury. The machines were efficient and the original ones had been impersonal. People had found them frightening so some genius had programmed in a bedside manner.

Again on my lunch break I came to Ellen's ward. There was a new nurse on duty, taking the usual physical care of patients which fell outside the abilities of the machine. Puffing up pillows, taking away bodily wastes, adding or removing blankets, that kind of thing. In all honesty, the blanket thing wasn't necessary. The ambient temperature was controlled by the machine in each cubicle, but sick people were soothed by the feel of a blanket. There were still some things you couldn't do automatically. Ellen still slept.

I came back at home time, hoping to see her propped up and smiling. The nurse had just left for the day and the machine was at the end of Ellen's cubicle. I crept up behind and watched the monitor. All her statistics scrolled across the screen. Vital signs, treatment options, prognosis. I often looked at my own patients' screens and the AI medics were always right on the ball.

The screen flashed with scrolling numbers then a sound came which I'd never heard before. I was beginning to suspect it never happened on the day shift, when the nurse was present. It sounded like a faint gong. On the screen there appeared details of medication prepared and the dosage. Then, what would be Ellen's final decision from the machine.

Patient no longer economically viable. Life terminated at 18:06 hours.

Lines in the Sand

They said Erik von Daniken was barmy when he suggested that alien races had previously visited Earth. It did seem far-fetched to suggest that the Nazca lines were runways for spacecraft. Why would they need runways? Nevertheless, as a young archaeologist, I was one of many people fascinated by the light markings in the desert which, as well as the 'runways', depicted strange, stylised animals and birds - a monkey with a ridiculously long curly tail - a flattened hummingbird - a massive spider. The markings themselves are shallow because there are never weather conditions such as winds or rainstorms which could erase them.

The first indication I had that there was something strange was the excavation where I found a small metal disc, perhaps three centimetres across. It was in a secure context and had been there for a very long time - as long as the lines in the desert. The disc had incised markings on it but it was a bright blue colour and nobody seemed to recognise what it was made of. The lab boys took it away and tested and retested it but came up with the answer that the material was not known on earth. It was an entirely new compound and it didn't sound as if they really knew what its constituents were.

Our group was still finding scraps of metal, fabric and

something that resembled ceramic on this site. They bore no resemblance to anything else we know today. The lab people have tried to find how to replicate these materials but they are on a loser. They are not just alien artefacts, they are made of metals refined from alien ores. The big questions are, did the visitors leave? Why did they make the lines in the sand?

I was as full of questions as any scientist would be, and one of the local academics who tried to answer them from her own interest in the phenomenon was Beatriz. We worked together and as we became closer we realised we were falling in love. As we were arranging our wedding and Beatriz was deciding on her trousseau, she removed a small silver necklet from her jewellery box.

"Don't you think this will look perfect against my dress?" she asked. I looked closely at it. Something about it made me shiver, though whether with excitement or fear, I couldn't say. I tried to sound casual.

"Where did you get it? It's delightful. Unusual though, don't you think?"

"It was my great grandmother's," she said, "so I know it's old. No idea how old though. I'm glad you like it. I'll wear it for the wedding then."

The incised glyphs on the necklet were identical to those on the blue disc - and very few people knew about that. They had to have been copied but the disc had been buried for thousands of years. It caused me to wonder if this was a traditional pattern in Peru. I asked Beatriz but she was sure she hadn't seen it anywhere else.

I couldn't keep this to myself and told her my suspicions. When I put them into words they sounded outrageous. "You don't suppose your family met with the alien visitors way back in the past, do you?"

"It's possible. It's even possible we were their offspring!" she laughed - then her face straightened as she saw my shocked look.

"I just meant, could they have settled here? Made their big 'HELP' sign in the desert, but not been rescued? Could they even have interbred with the locals?" she explained. I had to admit that it sounded beyond unlikely. Even some earth creatures that were closely related genetically couldn't produce offspring capable of reproduction.

How badly did we want to find out? Beatriz was excited. I was afraid. We discussed it and decided to approach one of our friends in the labs. Jim could test Beatriz's DNA privately for us. The results would be guaranteed not to go into any database. "Oh let's go for it, or we'll always wonder," she said.

It was a long wait for those results and it felt even longer. We went to the lab to find out. We knew we'd both be so full of questions but with Jim on hand to interpret we stood a chance of making some sense of it all. Beatriz's eyes were alight but I felt as if I'd swallowed a stone. I wasn't sure what I wanted the result to be. Jim produced a print-out and started to point to DNA markers and to explain their significance.

"But these here," he said with a wrinkled brow, "no idea what these are. It's as if human DNA has been mixed up with something else." He caught the significant look we exchanged. "That's what you're thinking, isn't it?" he asked. "That Beatriz has a distant relation from the stars?"

Very few local people have had DNA tests but we've had one or two cousins and slightly more distant members of my wife's family tested and the same few strange markers are present. Do we tell anyone? As a scientist I've always valued knowledge for its own sake. I could never have imagined keeping results a secret. Beatriz wants the three of us to publish a scientific paper on the subject but I'm afraid my wife and now my unborn child will be treated as specimens -

as creatures to be studied in a lab, rather than fellow humans.
I don't know what to do.

Lovesick

Cara usually tried to sit near the blond boy on the school bus. She fancied him rotten. She used to sit behind him and sigh. Her mum had noticed she'd gone off her food and her best friend Emma, not the most sensitive girl in the class, was aware that Cara was not herself. She was totally mopey and maungy.

"What's the matter with you, Cara? You've got a face as long as a wet Whit Week!"

Cara tried to make light of it but Emma was persistent. Eventually as she watched her friend gazing and sighing on the school bus she realised what was the matter.

"It's him, isn't it? That Jason lad? He's well fit but I wouldn't go overboard myself. How long have you fancied him?"

"Oh, dunno. Maybe a couple of weeks. I think he's just gorgeous. He makes me tingle in places I didn't know I had a few weeks back! But, Emma, he doesn't even see me. He doesn't notice I exist. I could stand on my head in front of him and wave my knickers in the air and he'd just crane his neck to see round me!"

Emma thought for a while. "Leave it with me," she said. "I'll sort something out."

Emma was a deep thinker (at least, she thought she was).

She was a believer in natural magic and certainly felt that women should take fate into their own hands. She decided to do some research into love potions. Google kept giving her references to websites that wanted to sell her spells but she wanted to do her own magics. Or should that be Magicks?

She discovered that one of history's most attractive women was Cleopatra. She must have had some secret to her success.

"Probably 'cos she was stinking rich," sighed Cara.

"Can't just be that though," Emma said. "There's loads of beautiful and rich women around but she's gone down in history. She's got to have had something special."

She returned to her researches. Eventually she read that Cleopatra drank pearls dissolved in wine. She told Cara about it.

"Blimey! See, stupidly rich. What did I tell you?"

"No, listen," Emma insisted. "Mark Anthony was talking about some rich person's banquet where Cleo took her earrings out and tossed them in a wine glass and said, 'You want rich, matey? Well watch this,' and she knocked it back. Mark Anthony was crazy over her. Stands to reason, dunnit?"

Cara wasn't convinced but she was sick of trying to catch Jason's eye. She had to do something or she'd just die. The problem was, she was obviously nowhere near as well off as Cleopatra and she didn't have wine, let alone pearls, hanging around. Emma said she'd read on a couple of websites that you probably had to use vinegar because people had tried it and it took yonks to get a pearl to disappear in a glass of wine. And anyway, old fashioned wine was really sour so vinegar wasn't far off.

"Wine, vinegar... It's not going to make a scrap of difference if we haven't got any pearls, is it?" moaned Cara miserably. "Jason's never even going to know I exist!" Even his name made Cara sigh.

"Oh pull yourself together, girl!" her mum snapped as

once again Cara walked around the living room in a daze.

"Have you got any pearls, Mum?" she asked, rather hopelessly.

"Who d'you think I am? Royalty?"

"No, but have you?"

"What d'you want pearls for? They were old fashioned even back in my day. I did have a pair of stud earrings once. Your dad bought me them when we were courting. I don't know what happened to them though. I think I lost one of them." That was all Cara needed to know. While her mum was distracted with the telly, she went into her parents' bedroom and raked about in her mum's bedside cabinet. Result! One pearl earring. Like that girl in the book. Come to think of it, she had a soppy, love-struck look about her too. Cara felt her pulse quicken. There could be something in this love potion thing of Emma's after all.

Emma started to make the potion. She had a feeling she was missing something. A real white witch would have a silver goblet, surely, but think what that would look like after soaking in vinegar. It would go all black and horrible. She ought to have a knife too. She'd read that somewhere. And you needed to say some words? A spell of some kind? She'd just have to do her best.

Well, wine was impossible, but it even took a couple of days to make much impression on the pearl in white wine vinegar. Even the distracted Cara could see that something was happening to it though. After a week it was a few gritty grains in the bottom of the glass. Emma strained it into a small screw-top bottle for her suffering friend.

"I don't know how much you have to drink," she said. "It sounds like Cleopatra just knocked it all back. I'll meet you at the bus stop and you can swallow it then. Better take it all. Then when you get on the bus, go right up to him. Say hello. Make sure he sees you."

The next morning, just before the school bus was due, Emma unscrewed the top from her home-made love philtre and passed it to Cara, who trustingly put her head back and gulped it down.

"Bloody hell Em! It's gross! Oh, god that's just mingin'!"

"Shush, stop your moaning. Here's the bus. Up those stairs, chop-chop. And stand in front of him. And smile!"

Cara staggered her way up the bus stairs, looking and feeling horribly queasy. No wonder they called this 'feeling lovesick.' She stood in front of the dreamy blond Jason, gave him a winning but wonky smile, then threw up a shower of vinegary vomit straight into his lap. Oh, hell. She was lovesick alright. Emma claimed afterwards that her 'spell' had been successful. Cara couldn't deny that Jason had noticed her!

Magda

"Gotcha!"

The old woman leapt out from behind a holly bush and grabbed Hansi and his sister Greta by their wrists. She dragged them towards a huge wooden box with a door composed of vertical metal bars.

"A cage!" whispered Greta, wide-eyed.

"I'll fatten you up," said the old woman. She had the classic look - bent back, squinty eyes and several hairy warts.

"A witch," said Hansi as the crone scuttled off into her cottage.

She returned shortly with a plate of bread and butter and a jug of milk. "Tuck in," she croaked, and gazed myopically around.

Hansi shrugged and began to eat. "Come on, we might as well eat it up. It's good!"

"I've read a story like this," said Greta. "This wicked witch fattens up two children for the oven, but they trick her. When she checks how fat their fingers are they push a stick through the bars and she thinks they're still all thin and bony."

"Where are we going to find a stick?" asked Hansi, shoving his hands in his pockets where he found - not a stick, that would be too easy, wouldn't it? He found a stub of pencil.

Ten minutes later, Magda scurried out. "Finger!" she

snapped. "Stick out your finger!" Hansi poked the pencil out and pulled it back rapidly when the witch shrieked, "Lummie! The poor child's got a bad case of dendritis. He's turning into a tree!" She opened the cage and, looking Greta straight in the eye, she winked. "Better plant you in some decent soil and let you grow," she continued, dragging Hansi by the wrist again. She grabbed a spade from the vegetable plot and dug a small hole which she made Hansi stand in. The soil didn't even cover his boots. She let her hands travel over the pencil, tutted, then felt up towards his furry hat. Again she shrieked. "Gaah! He's already got a bad case of squirrels!"

The sun was setting now. It was Christmas Eve and their parents would be frantic. Magda again pulled them behind her as she hurried them into her cottage. "Play along," she whispered.

Soon the children were seated in front of toast and hot milk. "Sorry about that," said Magda. "I'm trying to get them to award me honourable retirement."

"Who?"

"The Worshipful Company of Crones. The new Chief Crone hates me. I'm pretending I've lost me marbles but I know she's doubtful. She even criticised my cackle. I started finding bottles of Benylin on the doorstep. I don't want to end up in the Gleeful Guild of Grannies. Who'd want knitting and milky tea when you could have orgies and gin?"

"Orgies? Really?"

"We talk about them," she said in a wistful voice. "Anyway, off you go. Your parents will be worrying."

"Thanks for the toast. It was lovely," Greta said.

"Yes... Very Crispness." An odd remark, but it was the nearest Magda dared utter to a seasonal greeting. Crones have ears.

Hate

It's a strong word, isn't it? And do we really mean it? I hear it so often these days that I think it's lost its true meaning. 'I hate rhubarb' means I don't like the flavour or texture. 'I hate these drunken louts in town on a Friday night' means I feel uncomfortable watching them. 'I hate foreigners' usually means I'm scared of anyone different from me. But I once truly felt hatred. It scared me shitless.

My first flat was at the top of a four storey block. I chose it because it was fairly cheap, so I could save for a deposit for a small house. It was also, being central, very handy not only for work but for the pubs and clubs I'd drop into of an evening. There were four flats to a floor so only sixteen altogether. I was in number sixteen. At number fifteen was a young couple, Jack and Amy. Not ideal neighbours, they were the door-slamming, yelling and loud music variety, but I was on the opposite side of the block so it was usually tolerable.

They had a baby. Bonny little thing they called Lily. At first Amy would parade her round the block to the shops in her little pram. Later, the shouting increased. The baby cried and Jack yelled back at it – almost as if it were a conversation. It used to worry me the way the crying would stop so suddenly. I noticed Amy sporting the occasional black eye and, on one occasion, she limped badly, using the pram to support her weight. There was violence in that household. Violence against a young woman and a tiny child. In my world, this isn't acceptable.

I started going out with Claire shortly afterwards and we'd often end up at my place at the end of the evening. Whatever time we climbed the stairs - it didn't have a lift – there was shouting, swearing and the crashing of thrown things from number fifteen. Claire was worried about Amy and her baby. I was myself, but how do you intervene? I tried ringing the police who weren't keen to come to a noisy 'domestic dispute'. I wanted social services to visit. They had no grounds to, they said.

One Friday night, quite late on, we heard Jack coming in. He'd obviously been drinking. Claire went to look through the little spy-hole in my door, and said he could barely walk. He banged on his own front door with his fists and the language was ripe. I blushed at the thought of my girlfriend listening to this.

"Come away, Claire," I said. "It's nothing to do with us."

Soon, though, it was. A thumping on my door, screaming, a sobbing voice, led me to unlock it. Amy stood before me, in her nightwear, blood covering the lower part of her face. Her nose was bleeding, her lip was split, and unwashed makeup gave her a panda-eyed look. She was a mess, and she was almost incoherent as I tried to get out of her what was the matter.

"Lily!" she cried. "He's shaking Lily! Just 'cos she won't settle down. I told him, but he just smacked me in the face. Help me!"

Claire gathered Amy in her arms and shepherded her into my flat. We exchanged looks. "Police?" she asked. I nodded.

I went to Jack's door and banged on it. "Jack! Come on, mate. Let me in."

I won't tell you what he told me to do. I think some of it is physically impossible. A torrent of cursing and crudity poured out of their flat. And still he had that poor baby in his hands, if Amy were to be believed.

"Let me in, Jack. Maybe we can stop her crying. That's what you want, isn't it?" I felt like one of those negotiators you see talking terrorists off aeroplanes. I deliberately kept my voice low, soothing and non-confrontational. The tirade of abuse continued, together with the sound of furniture being smashed and crockery being dashed against floors or walls. God knew what state that place was in now, and the baby. That poor little baby – she was screaming worse than ever.

I tried their door. It wasn't locked. I was greeted by a great roar and before I had time to enter, Jack rushed out onto the landing, breathing beery, smoky breath into my face, making me step back, toward the head of the stairs. He had baby Lily in one hand. In fact, he had hold of her by the tiny, greying vest she was wearing.

"Let me have the baby, Jack. She can stay with us tonight. Give you a good night's sleep, eh?"

"I know what you're doing!" he slurred. "Got my woman in there too, have yer?" More ripe language. Please, God, let Amy have got through to the police. Let there be some help on its way. Someone who was used to this sort of drunken bully.

My own door opened at that point, and Amy stood there, quivering with fear. "Don't hurt her, Jack," she pleaded. "Let me have her. I'll settle her down."

At that, Jack's eyes lit. He pushed past me and dangled the now limp baby over the bannister – out over the four storey drop of the stair-well. Amy screamed. I heard Claire gasp. The tiny body was dangling, face down, over a sheer drop. Jack was holding her by the scruff of the vest and watching Amy's reaction, a nasty sneer on his face. This child was just a tool to hurt his partner. The vest was one of those with poppers under the crotch, and as he shook her, I heard one snap undone. Two more and the baby's little, bruised body would simply slide out and down onto the concrete far below.

We both heard a bang from down the stairs. The outside door had been opened and had slammed shut. I sidled toward the drop and looked down. A police officer, thank God. He started to climb the stairs.

Jack's bloodshot eyes swivelled in panic. I took the chance of the distraction and lunged for the baby, grabbing her by the front of the vest. A horrible tussle took place. If she fell just onto the floor here, on the landing, it would probably kill her. I had to get her away from her father.

One glance down the stairwell told me the police officer was watching as he laboured up the stairs. His jaw fell as he must have seen a crazed man gesturing with the body of a tiny baby. I even saw him reach out into the space between the turn of the stairs. Perhaps he thought he could catch the child if she fell.

He was now just below our flight, but panting hard. I kept hold of Lily's vest and, with my other hand, I made a fist and crashed it into Jack's nose. Let him see what it felt like for Amy. He swore, staggered back and let go of the child. I could have stopped then, but I didn't. I knew what hate meant. I passed Lily to her shaken mother.

This miserable apology for a man had his hands over his face, catching the welling blood. Without a thought for the police witness, I kneed him in the groin, then, as he doubled up, I kicked his feet out from under him. He tumbled down the stairs, hitting every one of the concrete steps as he did. Sadly, he only made it to the first landing, but I could see from the angle of his left foot that he wouldn't be running away.

It hit me what I'd done. I'd felt so much hatred for another man that I could be accused of grievous bodily harm, or even attempted murder. And the witness was an officer of the law.

I realised the officer hadn't attempted to catch Jack in his headlong tumble. He'd stepped back out of the way to allow him to fall as far as the landing, where he was now groaning and spewing up some of his earlier lager and curry.

I could hear the girls behind me cooing over Lily. The door shut with a click as they took her inside.

I looked at the policeman as he finally reached my landing. What could I say? He had me bang to rights. He'd seen what happened. "Suppose it's no use saying sorry?" I asked, as I held my hands out, expecting to be handcuffed.

"Nowt to be sorry for, lad. He was resisting arrest, wasn't he?" At least I wasn't alone in my feelings that this man didn't deserve much in the way of mercy.

So don't go telling me you hate bananas or the Tories or boy racers. Until you've wanted to kill a man, you don't know what hatred is.

Is It True?

George came home on the last school day before the Christmas holidays looking anything but happy. His mum, Sarah, was preparing vegetables at the sink and turned to greet him.

"George, what's up, love?"

"Mum, some big kids told me and my mates that there's no such person as Father Christmas! Is it true, Mum? Is he real or is he made up?"

Sarah quickly dried her hands on her apron and knelt in front of her distraught young son. "Look at me, George. There's an old saying, 'Those who don't believe, don't receive.' You always get presents, don't you? Some from us and some from Father Christmas. I hope those big boys don't get any. That'll teach them not to try to ruin Christmas for other children."

George scuffed his damp nose with the sleeve of his school sweater. Sighing, Sarah kissed him on the top of the head. "Run upstairs and get changed. Fetch me your uniform down and it can go in the washer."

"But is it true? Is Father Christmas real?"

"You keep believing and we'll see what happens on Christmas morning, shan't we?"

On Christmas Eve, just as George switched on the tree

lights, his dad came home, looking terrible. He swept past his son with a thin smile and a nod and went into the kitchen.

Sarah faced him, hands on hips. "Will. Is it true? I met Barry in the post office just as I came out of work. He said the factory's closing down in the new year and everyone's being made redundant. Is it true?"

"It's true, love. I found out last week but I couldn't face telling you."

"I'd find out soon enough, wouldn't I? What'll we do?"

Will slumped onto a kitchen chair. "I dunno. The dole queue is going to be massive. Everyone will be looking for a new job. It's hopeless."

"We'll get by. I can take on more hours. We'll have to tighten our belts but we'll manage. You'll get another job, love. You're young, strong, bright. Something will come up."

Will's jaw clenched. He looked up at Sarah, his chin jutting as though he expected a blow. "We're gonna be really strapped for cash, Sarah. Really strapped. Good job all George's presents are paid for. But while I've got a bit of change in my pocket I'm off to drown my sorrows. Don't wait up."

He strode to the back door, grabbed his jacket and went out into the night.

"And Merry Christmas to you, too," Sarah mumbled, stifling tears in case George came through.

"Where's Dad?" George asked as they started their meal.

"He had to go out, love. He said not to wait up for him. But we want a nice early night, don't we? Father Christmas doesn't come till you're asleep, remember."

Finally George was in bed and sleeping soundly, allowing Sarah to bring his presents from her wardrobe and pop them under the tree. He was waiting for Father Christmas; she went to her own bed to wait for her husband, though she knew she wouldn't like the state he was in. He rarely went out on his own, just with the purpose of getting drunk so she knew his Christmas morning would be subdued.

She must have fallen asleep because she jerked awake at the sound of a dull thud on the front door, followed by rattling and scuffling. He couldn't even get the key in the lock! She turned over. There was no point in going down. No point in starting a row.

***

Will had staggered out of the pub when they finally locked up. He was swaying, the scenery was swaying, and not always in time with one another. He threw up in the shrubbery surrounding the car park. That made him feel slightly better for the moment, if you didn't count the evil taste in his mouth. He banged and knocked into trees, litter bins and lampposts as he rattled his way home.

He turned into his own garden and, attempting to avoid falling into his own privet hedge, he took a staggering sideways walk over the flower beds. Hell, he'd be in trouble for that in the morning. Still, how much worse could things get? No job, a wife, a child and a mortgage. He was stuffed anyway.

He fetched up at the front door with a thud. Holding onto it with one hand, he tried to get the key into the lock with the other. It kept missing. Damn it. He held himself up against the door with his left shoulder and head, and used both hands to poke the key at the lock-plate. Eventually, using his left hand as a kind of funnel, he managed to guide the stupid key into the lock. The door swung back and he fell into the hall. Bloody hell! All that mud. Where'd that come from?

Shh. He tiptoed into the living room and by the dying light of the open fire, he could see he'd tracked mud in from the garden all over the hall and the lounge carpets. He bent to take off his shoes before things got any worse, and fell over, narrowly missing the fire. Strangely the fireguard had been moved away. Oh God. Christmas. That was it. Poor George, having a useless dad like him.

Snack. That's what he needed. He was suddenly starving. A mince pie, that was the ticket. Then, carrying the filthy shoes, he stumbled into the kitchen. He put the shoes by the back door and filled a glass with water. That should help. Plenty of water to prevent a hangover, they always said.

As he made his erratic way up to bed, he could feel the water sloshing in his stomach. Might not have been such a good idea. He scrambled out of his clothes and crept into bed in his underwear.

***

"Mum, Mum, he's been!" George leapt onto their bed, worming his way between his parents. "Father Christmas has been. And Mum, it's all true!"

"I told you it was." Sarah smiled and ruffled his hair, while his father groaned and turned over with a gust of breath that smelt like paint-stripper.

"Mum, he came. He's real! He left his footprints from the front door to the fireplace – and Mum! He ate the mince pie!" George's face fell slightly as he continued, "but he didn't drink the sherry."

"If Father Christmas drank a glass of sherry at every house in the world he'd have a bad stomach and a headache by Christmas morning, wouldn't he?"

"Suppose."

"Come on, get dressed and we'll go and get a bacon butty and open those presents." Will groaned again.

Things seemed bad now but, like a hangover, they could only get better. Later, Sarah came in with a mug of strong coffee and a couple of painkillers. Will wouldn't want much more than that for his Christmas dinner.

And that *was* true!

Acknowledgments

My thanks go to Aly Shaw for the cover image. Also, as always, to Jonathan Hill, who turned that painting into a cover, and provided editing and formatting services. And thanks to you, for reading it.

Six on the Beach and *Gemini* were first published in an anthology entitled *The Stars Will Shine Again.*

Dark Fires was first published in an anthology entitled *Criminal Shorts*, published by the UK Crime Book Club.

ALSO BY THE AUTHOR

Novels
Top Banana
Long Spoon
The Flesh of Trees
The Sundowners
The Angel Monument
Becca
Through His Eyes
Old Haunts

Novellas
Ravenfold
Message in a Bottle
Souls Disturbed: Three Supernatural Tales
Beneath the Ink

Short Stories
Stir-up Sunday
The Novice's Demon
Muriel's Bear
Tales from Daggy Bottom (a collection)

Collaborations
Beyond 100 Drabbles (with Jonathan Hill)
Is it Her? (with Jonathan Hill)

Printed in Great Britain
by Amazon

30833923R00079